It Began As a Quarrel in a Local Bar . . .

I stepped off the stool, the bottle in my hand. I said, "I'm going to report this." I had lifted the bottle up, to sip it, when Curly reached a hand toward my shoulder. It was his left hand and his right hand was balled.

I backhanded the bottle into the side of his jaw. I heard Jackie squeal and then something crushed my solar plexus and I went down next to the stool. Curly had swung a left hand faster than the eye.

I was sick and dizzy, but my groping hand found one leg of my bar stool and I came up swinging it. It caught Curly in the hip and he yelped, and came in before I could swing it back.

It was my lucky day. He got tangled in the rungs as I retreated and he started to fall. And I put all of my two hundred and twenty pounds into the right hand I threw at his exposed chin . . .

DAY OF THE RAM

William Campbell Gault

CHARTER BOOKS, NEW YORK

A condensed version of this
book appeared in the June, 1957
issue of *Omnibook*.

This Charter Book contains the complete
text of the original edition.
It has been completely reset in a typeface
designed for easy reading, and was printed
from new film.

DAY OF THE RAM

A Charter Book / published by arrangement with
the author

PRINTING HISTORY
Random House edition / July 1956
Bantam edition / August 1957
Charter edition / October 1988

ISBN: 1-55773-091-1

Charter Books are published by The Berkley Publishing Group,
200 Madison Avenue, New York, New York 10016.
The name "CHARTER" and the "C" logo are trademarks
belonging to Charter Communications, Inc.

PRINTED IN THE UNITED STATES OF AMERICA

10 9 8 7 6 5 4 3 2 1

For the Milwaukee gang:

Brown and Sternig
Mapes and Kruger
Woolgar and Peterson

THE MAN NEXT to me said, "They should have old Water-buckets out there. The Bears never gave him any trouble."

"The Bears give everybody trouble," I said.

"Not Waterbuckets. Not even the Dutchman." The man shook his head. "This bum Quirk, where'd they pick him up?"

I didn't answer. Who wants to argue with a Ram fan? From the other side of me, Jan said, "It's only an exhibition game. Who cares about exhibition games? Wait'll the season starts."

She's an expert too, now. Last year she didn't know a football from a golf ball, but if there's anything you want to know about the Rams, just ask her. She's got the answers.

In case you don't know about the Rams, Waterbuckets means Bob Waterfield, long since retired, and the Dutchman is Norm Van Brocklin, only recently retired. Great quarter-backs, both of them. And the T-formation without a great quarterback is like a car without a motor; it may look beautiful, but it simply won't go.

We were sitting in the Coliseum, Jan and I, on a sun-filled September day, watching the Rams play the Bears. It was the middle of the third quarter and the Rams had just called for a time out, and well they might. For the Bears were leading 24 to 7, and they had a first down on the Ram nineteen-yard line.

And though the Rams had lost four straight exhibition games, fifty-three thousand people sat in the Coliseum with us, throwing insults at Chicago's big, bad Bears. How many came because they loved the Rams and how many because they hated the Bears there is no way of knowing. Hatred of the Bears is just a hungover habit from the forties; they're as clean as any team in the League, today. And cleaner than some I could name, but won't.

Time was in again, and the Bears' great fullback, Dane, was coming around this end on a naked reverse. But Les Richter hadn't been fooled. They met on the line of scrimmage and a man from Glendale later claimed the impact had cracked a mirror over his mantel. It might have just been a gag, of course.

In any event, Dane went down and the ball went scooting and Robustelli dove and it was Rams' ball, first and ten on their own nineteen.

The man next to me let out a yip and Jan was screaming, "Go, go, go—" but Dane was still on the ground, absolutely motionless.

A respectful silence; nobody hates the Bears *that* much. Then Dane moved a leg as the trainer came out, and Dane stirred as the trainer bent over him. And a few seconds after that he was on his feet and being helped off the field, and the stands cheered him lustily. It's not any one Bear who is hated, you see, it's *those damned Bears*.

And the man referred to as "that bum Quirk" was trotting out with the Ram offensive platoon.

And on the first play from his own nineteen, that bum Quirk went back to fling one, fading almost to the goal line. If you follow college ball, you'll probably wince at that. But this isn't college ball. This game is played by experts who *like* the game.

Quirk faded and Boyd streaked. When he was three steps beyond the safety man, Boyd turned and there was the ball, big as a balloon. And nobody in America is going to catch Boyd from behind.

And Jan was screaming and pounding my shoulder and I turned to the man next to me and said with quiet dignity, "That bum Quirk looked pretty goddamned good on that one, didn't he?"

"Eaaaa," the man said. "It was Boyd, all Boyd. You got to follow the Rams to understand about that. You follow the Rams?"

I am a modest man. I merely smiled. But Jan is handy in a spot like that. Jan said coolly, "You are talking to Brock, the Rock, Callahan, mister."

The man stared at her and then at me. And then he said,

"By God, you are. What are you doing up here? The way the Rams need guards, what are you doing up here?"

"Enjoying the game," I said. "My playing days are behind me."

"Oh, yeah," he said. "I remember. You're a cop or something now, right? You helped nail those two hot-rod hoodlums, right?"

"Right as rain," I agreed, and handed him my card. "Any time you need discreet investigation at moderate rates, I hope you'll remember me."

He shook his head and smiled. "The Rock? Who'll ever forget the Rock?"

I tried not to look smug and Jan chuckled. Les Richter kicked the point-try and the score was 24 to 14, favor of the Bears.

And there were still six minutes to go in the third quarter.

I played against the Packers in Milwaukee one Sunday afternoon, when they had us 28 to 6 with twelve minutes to go. And then old Waterbuckets came in and tossed us to a 30 to 28 victory in those twelve minutes. I remember how those fans in Milwaukee sat in the stadium long after we were in the dressing room, refusing to believe what they had just seen.

And this sunny day, Quirk made like Waterfield. He came into his own that afternoon. At the end of the third quarter it was 24 to 21; Deacon Dan Towler had gone fifty yards to pay dirt on a fullback swingout.

And you could almost feel it way up there in the stands; Quirk had taken *command*. This was his ball game and it would go the way he willed it.

On the sidelines, the Bears' immortal George Halas sensed it, too, I'll bet. He was screaming at the officials and scowling at his boys, putting on a Halas side show that beats anything I've ever seen at a college game between the halves.

Quirk went back and the pass patterns unfolded and the Rams could do nothing wrong that last quarter. And watching them, the new ones, the young ones, the eager ones, I saw some ghosts among them, ghosts who were probably now sitting in the stands, getting fat.

I saw Crazylegs and the Tanker and Long Tom Fears. I saw

Waterfield and Mr. Outside and Night Train. We'd had a team, and this was going to be another one, with Quirk finally finding himself.

The man next to me said, "Okay, I've been wrong before. That Quirk's going to be one of the great ones, isn't he?"

"You can make book on it," I said.

There may have been exhibitions to match Quirk's that afternoon, but I've never seen any. The Rams didn't punt once after that third quarter touchdown pass of his. Every time they were on the offensive, they moved the ball. In the last twenty-two minutes of the game, Quirk tried twenty-three passes. And completed twenty-one.

Even Halas subsided, standing quietly on the sidelines, knowing he was watching history being made. A quiet Halas; that, too, was history.

And then, on the last play of the game, as Quirk went back to throw another one, just for kicks, from his own eighteen, an enraged Bear line broke through the cup.

He'll get his lumps now, I thought. He'll get a present to take back to the locker room.

I was wrong. Quirk ran laterally, faking two tacklers right out of their socks. And then he cut sharply upfield.

And ran, untouched, eighty-two yards to the score.

And Les Richter kicked the point that made it 56 and that was the final, 56 to 24, Rams on top.

The screams had died, and in the great silence, as we all sat there still lost in the magic of it, Jan said, "The day of the Ram."

The man next to me frowned. "What's with her?"

"You've got me, mister," I answered. "She's kind of erudite."

"I was thinking of Quirk," Jan said. "*His* day, wasn't it? He'll never have a better one."

"That figures," my neighbor said. "You must have followed these Rams a long time, eh, lady?"

"For weeks," I said, and stood up. "God help the Forty-niners, huh?"

"God help 'em," my neighbor said solemnly. "This is our year."

Fifty-three thousand people filing out of the Coliseum, and it's usually noisy with chatter after a game. But today there was an unusual silence. It seemed to be an awed crowd.

And an anticipatory one; the Rams had been weak only at quarterback, but that's your team in the T. And now they had another great one, and God help the Forty-niners. And also the Packers and the Lions and the Colts and any Eastern Division teams who had been unfortunate enough to schedule them this year.

We were going down the ramp when Jan said, "He was like a god, like something from another world. He overshadowed this whole damned Coliseum. Where's he from?"

"Beverly Hills," I said. "And Princeton. Rich kid."

"Rich? And why should he play professional football, if he's so rich?"

I didn't answer.

About twenty seconds, and she said, "Golly, that was a dumb question, wasn't it? After what I saw today. The richest man in the world never had a day like that, did he?"

I shrugged. "It depends on what you want, I suppose. Tommy Manville has probably had some fine days in his career."

"You're being vulgar again," she said.

Again I said nothing.

I opened the door of my flivver for her and then went around to climb in behind the wheel. I turned the radio on and sat back. I wasn't about to buck that traffic for half an hour.

Jan lighted a cigarette and asked softly, "Do you miss it, Brock?"

"Mmmmmm—No. No, not really. It's a rough grind, kid, from Redlands in July to the Pro Bowl game in January. And guards don't get the—adulation that backs do. No, I don't miss it."

"You're lying," she said, "but I suppose it's only rationalization. You're over the hump, aren't you? And that knee—"

"The knee doesn't bother me much. How's business?"

"In a lull. Don't change the subject."

"I'm over the hump," I said. "My business is in a lull, too."

"No Glenys Christophers have dropped in?"

That was my first case, and if you want to read about it, the book's still available. I said, "Nobody has dropped in for two weeks. But the rent's reasonable, considering the location."

"Couldn't you wrestle or box or something?"

I turned to stare at her. "I couldn't box and I wouldn't wrestle. Why? What's with you, as the man said?"

"That man, that god, that Quirk—the way they all screamed his name. After you've once known that, how can you desert it?"

"I never knew it, honey. If I'm real lucky and the man opposite me is temporarily asleep, I might get him out of the way. And in doing that, I might make a little hole. And if the back is fast enough and the secondary is taken care of, he might go through that little hole to six big points. And he will be a hero, but who will think of Brock Callahan, who made the little hole?"

"That man next to you remembered you. I meet people every day who remember you."

"Not every day."

"Well, quite often. And you don't smoke and you drink only beer, mostly. I mean—what are you saving yourself for?"

I smirked. "I have some insatiable lady friends."

Silence, while she glared at me. The radio played "Let Me Go, Lover" and I had a feeling Jan might let one go from left field. She has before.

I said quietly, "I apologize. But, kid, get off my back."

"I apologize, too," she said. "I'm—still all wound up, I guess. Childish, isn't it? I see what the sports writers mean now by 'autumn madness,' though. It's a fascinating game, isn't it? It has grace and courage and quickness and cunning and a hundred minor miracles. It's . . ."

It's a lot of things she didn't know about and never would. It's drill, drill, drill until you want to turn in your suit. And it's a knee in the groin and the cleated foot in the teeth and vicious sports writers and only average pay, too. It's a lot of things you don't see on Sunday afternoons from the stands.

Traffic was thinning out; I started the motor of the flivver and eased out into the traffic on Vermont. The Sunday drivers were out in full force and the going was slow.

The radio was giving the score of the Ram-Bear game now. And then the other scores. The Giants had beaten the Eagles. The revitalized Packers were going strong; they'd won their fifth straight exhibition game, walloping the Cardinals 38 to 10. Under Blackburn, the Packers could come back to glory.

In the old days this had been a three-team league: the Packers, the Bears and the Giants. They won all the titles; there were teams in the league who hadn't beat the Packers once in twenty years. And then the Lions and the Browns and the Forty-niners and the Rams had come to power and any one game was a toss-up.

And a quarterback like Johnny Quirk could take the Rams from door-mat status to a title. This would be the year of the Ram.

"You certainly look smug and happy," Jan said. "Business in a lull and us in a traffic jam—what makes you so happy?"

"Johnny Quirk."

We were stopped for a light and there was an Imperial in the lane next to us. The man behind the wheel looked over, smiled and waved. Jan waved back.

"Nice friends you have," I said.

"I did his house for him," Jan said. "His name's Rick Martin. He's in the investment business." She paused. "Wait, you were being sarcastic—do you know him?"

"I know him. Enrico Martino. And he's not in the investment business."

The light changed and we moved on. "Well!" Jan said. "Aren't we indignant? What business is he in?"

"I think he started as a pimp and went into stags from there. He claims to be a gambler now. Did you go out with him?"

"Not that it's any of your business, but I did, a few times. I think you're wrong about him. He's gentle and amusing and he has excellent taste."

"He's a slimy bastard," I said, and swung onto Wilshire, just missing the front fender of a gunning Buick.

Silence. I glanced at Jan and saw her grimness. Here we go again, I thought. Silence, growing and deepening.

And then she said, "You're so clean and noble. You're such a prize. You're no Eagle Scout, Brock Callahan. Don't be so quick to judge."

Nothing from me. Jan is a wonderful girl, small and neat and beautifully built and talented and entertaining. But though I like to tell myself I am tolerant and adult, I was brought up in Long Beach and some of it still lingers. And since our first meeting, on the Mira case, I hate to see Jan with another man. Except for that we rarely fight.

Silence. The Ford went moving along in the Wilshire traffic and the setting sun glinted off the chrome and windshields of all the cars and I pulled the visor down and squinted ahead, ingoring her.

Finally she said, "It was such a glorious day, but you've ruined it. It isn't the first time, Brock. I don't think we should see each other any more."

Nothing from me.

"I don't want to be spiteful about it," she went on in her patient way, "but you're vulgar and tactless and insensitive."

I didn't argue.

"We just don't seem to have any common meeting ground," she said thoughtfully.

Common enough, I thought. But said nothing.

"I have a *mind,* too, you know," she said with more heat.

I nodded.

"And a number of clients think I have impeccable taste. As a matter of fact, a number of my clients consider me the best interior decorator in Beverly Hills."

"I'll bet you are, too," I said. "Should we eat at Milton's?"

"I have a dinner engagement," she said.

I glanced at her. "With who?"

"It's 'whom,' not 'who.' With a friend."

"I'm a friend, Jan. I'm sorry I said what I did about Martino. He was probably at the game, and I don't like to see gamblers around games I like. And then, your going out with him—well, it burned me. He's not nearly good enough for you, Jan."

"Everybody gambles," she said evenly. "And I'm not marrying the man. I go out with all kinds of people and he was a lot nicer than some of them."

"Everybody gambles," I agreed, "but not professionally. I hate to see professional gamblers get interested in any decent sport. They've ruined boxing. Professionals of the caliber of Enrico Martino aren't satisfied with the percentages; they have to put in the fix."

"His name is Rick Martin; don't be a snob, Brock."

"All right, his name is now Rick Martin. And to hell with him. Do we eat at Milton's?"

"I don't know where I'm going to eat. I only know it's not going to be with you. We're not engaged, you know, Brock."

I sighed. "I know. All right. Tomorrow, could we be friends again?"

Silence. I cut around a tourist from Missouri and headed toward Sunset, toward the little cottage of Jan Bonnet, nestled in the canyon off Beverly Glen.

Not a word from her since my question. I turned up the narrow road that led to her house and heard the bark of the Doberman from the fenced yard next to Jan's. I parked and left the motor running.

"Some day he's going to get out," I said, "and chew me up. I wonder why he hates me so?"

She didn't answer that. She looked up at me thoughtfully. I reached over and stroked her tawny hair. It's sort of brownish-blond, as honest as the girl below it. Her eyes are brown and soft and difficult to mask with hardness, but she was trying to mask them now.

"Thanks for the afternoon," she said, and opened the door on her side.

"Aren't we friends?" I asked.

"I don't know, Brock. I don't want to talk about it now. Phone me tomorrow, if you want."

She got out and didn't look back. She went up the slope toward her house and the Doberman wagged his tail and tried to stick his nose through the wire netting of the fence. He loved Jan, the Doberman did, and I didn't blame him.

I guessed I loved Jan, too, in my vulgar and insensitive way.

The radio played an oldie, "Who's Sorry Now?" The Ford coughed and murmured as I headed it toward Westwood, which is home to me.

But on Westwood Boulevard, I didn't turn left, toward home. I kept going, toward the ocean, toward Malibu and a gang I knew would be waiting—a mild poker game among the old warriors, gridiron soldiers now over the hill. There would be memories and prophecies and beer. There would be some bragging and some heckling and the scarcely perceptible sadness of time-dimmed glory and faded newspaper clippings.

That's where I wound up Sunday, September fourth, the day that Johnny Quirk came to glory, the day the new team jelled, the day of the Ram.

MONDAY, SEPTEMBER FIFTH, dawned clear and dry. Outside my little apartment door, the *Times* lay fat and pompous and I took it in before putting the coffee on to perk.

Frank Finch devoted almost all his wordage to what he considered a breakdown of the Bear defenses in the last twenty-two minutes of the game. He couldn't have been more wrong; it had been an offensive miracle, not a defensive collapse. Cronin tried to get funny and failed as miserably as he always did. Well, Flaherty would see it; the *Examiner* really had the only major-league sports writer in town. Hyland devoted his column to his own spectacular career at Stanford and with the Marines, explaining that very few Big Ten athletes ever achieved officer status with the Marines. Because they hadn't played rugby.

Yesterday, on the Coliseum turf, a star had been born, a man who could possibly become one of the game's all-time greats. But the *Times* sport pages were concerned with other things, the greatness of U.C.L.A. and the appalling power-houses on its schedule, schools like San Diego State and East Compton College.

I ate my eggs and drank my coffee and thought back to last night and the seventeen dollars I had won. The talk had been Quirk, Quirk, Quirk last night, even among the losers. Usually the losers are only concerned with deal, deal, deal, but Johnny Quirk had been too big a discovery to make anything else worth discussing.

I bought an *Examiner* at the drug store near my office and opened it to Vincent X. Flaherty before I even looked at my mail.

Mr. Flaherty had seen it. From the first word to the last, his column was devoted to the new Ram quarterback. And his last sentence was: "*This will be one of the immortals.*"

I didn't read any of the other columnists; that was enough for me. I turned to the mail and there was nothing of importance. I got a paper cup of water from the water cooler and stood by the window, looking down at the traffic.

I'd opened the agency because there wasn't any other trade I could think of where I could do better. My dad had been a cop and as a Ram I'd known a hell of a lot of Los Angeles policemen. That wasn't much to bring to the profession, but some successful practitioners had originally brought less.

Of course, if one wanted to play the shadier angles of this game . . . Yes, of course. There were a number of ways to skin this cat and I'm not the most moral man in the world. But then again, I'm not the *least* moral either, I'm sure.

Behind me, the door opened and I turned to see a young man standing there. I thought, for a moment, that I'd gone simple.

Because it was Johnny Quirk.

"Am I seeing things?" I asked.

"You're Brock Callahan," he said.

I nodded. "And you're Johnny Quirk, and yesterday you were the best in the business. Man, you were great."

"Thanks," he said, and his smile was weak. "I guess I was pretty hot, all right. I hope it keeps up."

"So do I. So does every fan in town." Then I paused. "You seem nervous, Johnny. Something wrong?"

He nodded. He closed the door and came over to where I stood and handed me a piece of folded paper.

I put my half-empty cup of water on the desk before unfolding the paper.

The message was typed without salutation or signature. I read:

> *You're good enough to make the difference. And there's a lot of money to be made in this game if you're smart. We*

hope you're smart. We'll get in touch with you again.

I read it over twice and looked up to meet his anxious gaze. "Why did you bring this to me, Johnny?"

"You're a detective, aren't you? And a former Ram?"

I nodded. "But this is for the police. You should have taken it right to your head man Mr. Reeves and let him contact Commissioner Bell and get the police alerted. You knew that, didn't you, Johnny?"

"I knew if I was approached by gamblers, I had to report it, sure. This could be just a gag, though, couldn't it? What the hell would I want with money?"

I shook my head. "What we all want with it. You're not that naïve, boy."

"My dad's got more money than they're likely to have," he said. "I don't play this game for money."

"They don't know that, maybe."

"If they can read, they know it. I think it's a gag."

"No, you don't. Or you wouldn't have brought it to me. Tell me, why did you bring it to me, Johnny?" I nodded toward my customer's chair. "Sit down and tell me all about it.

He sat down, and I studied him. He didn't look much like a football player, but who does? He was slim, though fairly tall. The program carried him at a hundred and seventy-one pounds.

He took a deep breath and looked past me, at the window.

"Your folks?" I guessed. "You didn't want to worry your folks?"

"There's just Dad," he said. "Mom died when I was nine. No, it's not Dad. He doesn't scare. But my— There's a girl—I mean—"

"She doesn't like football?"

"Oh, she doesn't want *me* to play it. In high school, she thought it was great stuff. At Princeton, too, it made her a big girl at all the parties. But now, she says, it's time to put away these childish things."

I smiled. "You've gone with her since high school? That's

a pretty good record for these days."

He shook his head. "Off and on. We never went steady until the last couple of months. We're not engaged, yet, but . . ." He shrugged.

"Why aren't you engaged? Because of the football?"

He nodded. "Mostly. I thought maybe you could check the typewriter or whatever you fellows do and we could find out who the wise drip is and maybe—well . . ." He shrugged again.

"Maybe what?"

He frowned. "Golly, I don't know—I didn't think much beyond that." He smiled briefly. "You a Ram and all, and a guard, I suppose I figured you might work him over lightly."

"There must be more than one. This letter uses 'we.' "

"So do columnists, but one man writes the column."

I chuckled. "This isn't from a columnist. I doubt if even Hyland would send out a note like this. How did you get it? Have you the envelope?"

"It wasn't in an envelope. I found it folded on the seat of my car last night when I came out of a movie."

"It must have been someone who knew your car, then, or someone who followed you to the show. Is it an unusual car?"

He nodded. "It could be the only one in town. It's a bronze Ferrari with alligator upholstery."

Even in this town, that could be the only one. I stood up and said, "Let's go down to the station."

He stared at me. "Station? The police station?"

"Where else? Let's go boy. Right now."

He looked doubtful. Then he smiled. "It was just a gag, Brock. Some of the boys thought we'd have some fun with you, and—"

"Come on," I said. "You're a respected resident and they'll sit on it as long as they can. This is Beverly Hills, you know, not Los Angeles."

"But the Los Angeles police will have to know, won't they? And that means it will get in the papers and—"

"Maybe they won't have to know," I said. "We'll talk about that down at the station."

The Beverly Hills Police Station is on North Crescent Drive

and we walked over from my office. On the way I asked him, "Didn't you take your girl to the movie last night? Didn't she see the note?"

I thought he colored. "I—uh—wasn't with her last night."

"Who were you with? The police will want to know."

"A—girl. I'd rather not say."

"It might be important, Johnny. Your girl probably won't find out."

He shook his head. "I'm sorry I showed you the note."

I didn't argue with him. We went in and I asked for Lieutenant Remington and we were in his office within a minute.

He listened to the story and read the note, and then picked up a phone and asked the operator to get him Dan Reeves, the Ram manager.

While he waited for the connection, he said, "It could be a prankster or a crackpot, but there are strict rules on this kind of thing, Johnny. We don't want football to go the way boxing did."

Johnny nodded, looking faintly abashed.

Remington fiddled with a pencil. "Who was the girl, Johnny?"

Johnny shook his head.

Remington smiled. "Look, I won't tell your dad about—" Then he transferred his attention to the phone. "Dan? George Remington, Dan, and something rather important has . . ."

Monday, September fifth, that was and there was a long-distance phone confab with the National League Commissioner, Bert Bell, and then I was told by Remington that he really didn't need me at the moment, and he stayed with Johnny, trying to get the name of the girl.

I am a Beverly Hills businessman, but Johnny was a Beverly Hills *resident,* and there's a slight difference there, anyway a few million.

It was around noon and I went to the drug store for lunch. My most constant fan said, "I saved you some of those rye rolls. The short ribs are good, Brock."

"I'll have them," I said. "And the rolls and a glass of milk.

What kind of potatoes have you?"

"Au gratin, baked, French fried. They never should have let Pool go. Old Hamp wouldn't have lost all those exhibition games, right?"

"Baked," I said "and right. How about that Quirk?"

He made an "O" with thumb and forefinger. "A doll. A real Ram. This year, we go. Good-by, Detroit."

He brought over two rolls and three pats of butter. "Local boy, too. Needs the money like I need another head. Who'd have thought a Princeton punk would make it with the Rams, huh?"

"Some great boys have come out of the Ivy League," I said.

"Eah," he said. "You can have 'em. And the Big Ten, too. And seventeen points. I'll take the good old P.C.C."

I nodded. "Sure you will. Only they've been taken before, too often. Don't you watch the Rose Bowl games?"

He gave me a crushed look and went to get my short ribs. The Rose Bowl is a touchy subject out here.

I took my time eating and had another glass of milk.

I was still a little miffed at Remington's dismissal. My bad knee ached faintly and the memory of Martino came back—a slob in an Imperial, coming home from the game.

So, he was entitled; you don't need credentials to buy a ticket to a football game. All you need is the money, money, money . . .

"What did you say?" the counter man wanted to know.

"I didn't say anything."

"You were muttering. And scowling. Something wrong?"

I shook my head.

"It sounded like 'money' you were muttering about. What is that, a foreign word?"

I glared at him and he smiled at me and in a few seconds I smiled back. I couldn't lose him; he was one of the few remaining members of the Brock (the Rock) Callahan Fan Club.

There was nothing to draw me to the office; I walked over to a narrow shop on a nearby street. It was flanked by a pair of women's apparel stores. It had a wormwood front door and *jan bonnet* in uncapitalized black script on the shining show window. There were some metallic fabrics in the window and what looked like an ebony table with a marble top.

Jan was in soft green jersey today, with her hair up. She sighed and said, "Good afternoon. Something I can show you?"

"Pity? Tolerance? Ecstasy? What's your special today?"

She sniffed.

"Have fun last night?"

She nodded.

"I was thinking." I said, "that if you'd lend me the money, I could buy a ring and then we'd be engaged and we wouldn't have any reason to fight any more."

"To hell with you," she said.

"Don't be childish. Jan, we're friends and you know it. If we never kiss again, we're still friends. I may not like your friends and you may not like mine, but that doesn't change *us*."

She sighed again. She managed a small smile. "Sit down, Brock. It's been a bad morning. I had that Jethroe Ringlan all sold on the exquisite taste of Jan Bonnet and then he went to Les Hartley."

"Hartley, that queer?"

Jan's smile was bitter. "It seems Mr. Ringlan is, too."

I couldn't help it; I had to chuckle. "Taste and price and contacts mean nothing; you'll never beat that kind of competition, Jan."

"I would have netted seven thousand," she said. "Chuckle over that, muscle man."

"I'm sorry. I've had a bad morning, too. I've been snubbed by a crummy police lieutenant."

Her eyes widened. "Police? That means you have a case, you have a client?"

"I might have had. The police have taken it over."

"I'll bet I know why," she said quietly. "Because you insisted on going to the police. Old ethical Brock the Rock gets a customer and then leads him right down to the men who work for nothing. Aren't you supposed to be a *private* investigator? Isn't privacy what you sell?"

"Within the law, I sell it. Only within the law."

"You couldn't cut a close corner?"

"Not on this one I couldn't."

"What was so special about this one?"

"I can't tell you. It's privacy I sell."

She shook her head. "Oh, you—" She studied me. "Every trade, profession, business has it angles, Brock. Every intelligent operator within those categories learns the angles, or he gets out of the business. You don't have to be crooked to make a living, but it's also very juvenile to make a little plaster saint out of yourself."

"Yes'm," I said humbly.

"Well," she said briskly. "I can't sit around here. I have an appointment with a client."

I stood up. "I'll be seeing you, won't I?"

Her smile was a little too automatic. "Of course you will. We're friends."

I went out without any further words. One of the angles of the interior decorator's business is the kickback. The merchants send the bills direct to the client and then kick a part of the price back to the decorator. And the decorator charges for his or her—or its—services on top of that.

One of the angles of the private operative business is setting up phony infidelity situations for unhappy husbands or wives. And blackmail, and—

I bumped into something and saw that it was a small and angry man.

He glared at me. "Why don't you look where you're going?"

"Because I'm not sure where I'm going." I told him gently.

He went around me, shaking his head and muttering.

It was quiet in the office. The street is only one floor below, but the cars on the street are mostly new cars with big, fat tires. The little town of Beverly Hills has more Cadillacs than most states.

I made a target on a sheet of yellow paper and taped it to the filing cabinet. I sat in my swivel chair with a rubber band and a box of paper clips, improving my mind.

It wasn't long before I had the range and was hitting the

bull's-eye with one out of three. And none of them were completely missing the target.

I had emptied the box and was picking up the clips from the floor when my door opened to my second visitor of the day.

She was a girl of medium height and slim figure who could have been eighteen or twenty-five. I'm not good at guessing. She had black hair in one of those new short cuts and dark blue eyes. She looked from me to the clips on the floor and back to me.

"The box broke," I explained. "Could I be of service?"

"Are you Mr. Callahan?"

I nodded. "Won't you sit down?" I indicated the chair.

She stood where she was. "The Mr. Callahan who is a friend of John Quirk's?"

"I've met Johnny. Won't you sit down?"

She made no move. "John was here this morning, wasn't he?"

I frowned. "I—forget. I don't think it was this morning. I went back to picking up the paper clips.

"You needn't be rude," she said.

I straightened and gave her a steady look. "Nor you. Won't you sit down and tell me why you're here?"

She looked at the chair a moment and then went over to sit in it. She smoothed her skirt over her knees and said, "You don't look like a private detective."

"What do private detectives look like?"

"Oh, I thought they would look like men who would shoot girls in the stomach."

I laughed, and she smiled. I told her, "Those are the expensive kind. I'm more for the middle-class trade. Are you a friend of Johnny Quirk's?"

She nodded. "But I wish you wouldn't call him 'Johnny.' Why is he 'Johnny' to everybody all of a sudden?"

"Those things happen. Are you his—are you engaged to him?"

"I could be. I will be when he gives up this silly football mania of his."

I said nothing.

She said. "He came to see you this morning, didn't he?"

"Who told you that?"

"His father."

"Did his father tell you why?"

She shook her head, her eyes grave on mine. "You tell me."

"I can't, Miss—uh—"

"Curtis," she supplied, "Deborah Curtis. Why can't you?"

"Because he came in confidence; he trusted me. Don't worry about him, though. He's going to be all right. A number of important people are concerned with his welfare."

Some quiver in her fine chin and a scarcely perceptible shine of tears in the clear eyes. "He's in trouble, isn't he?"

I shook my head.

Her voice was shaky. "You're lying. That's another world, that world of John's. Women aren't permitted to enter, are they? You'd think there wasn't any world beyond those goal posts. It's like some crawling disease, isn't it?"

I shrugged. "Better men have had worse vices, Miss Curtis. John's a mighty fine boy, from all I've heard."

"Not fine enough to stay out of trouble, it seems."

"Nobody is," I said. "Nobody worth-while, anyway."

"Don't give me your locker-room homilies," she said fiercely. "I want to know about John."

"Do you, really? Then listen. He can be one of the greatest quarterbacks who ever played football in the toughest league in the world. *Despite* his money, he can be important on his own. And not only in Beverly Hills but in all the thousands of towns where sports are played. He can be one of the immortals instead of some puky little coupon-clipper and note shaver."

She sat rigidly in her chair, glaring at me. The tears were welling out of those blue eyes now and moving down her cheeks. I suddenly felt immensely sorry for her.

I said, "Five, six, seven years—can't you wait that long? You'll have him for the rest of his life. Can't the boys in the stands have him for a little while yet? He can make a lot of people happy doing what he's doing now."

She dried her eyes very carefully with a small yellow handkerchief. She sniffed and said, "I should have known better than to come here. You were a Ram, too, weren't you?"

"Yes'm."

"They're all crazy," she said, "all the ones I've met, anyway. You're no better than the others. I thought because you are older that—" She took a deep breath. "Men—"

I tried to think of something comforting to say, and failed. Who can explain about football to a nonbeliever? Women and professors can't seem to understand the importance of it.

She asked calmly, "You don't want to tell me anything, then?"

I shook my head. "Just don't worry, Miss Curtis. Your boy is going to be all right."

She stood up. "Did he tell you where he was last night?"

I lied with another shake of the head.

"Well," she said, "I'm sure he didn't go to a movie. Sorry to have troubled you, Mr. Callahan." She gave me her proud young back. She closed the door quietly behind her.

I went back to picking up the paper clips.

Two visitors in one day and not a dollar from either of them. I didn't have the true merchant's instinct. And that damned snooty Remington . . .

My phone rang, and it was that damned snooty Remington. I thought he sounded embarrassed, but it could have been because I was hoping he would.

He said, "Young Quirk seems to think a lot of you."

"I'm a Ram," I said.

"What was that?"

"Never mind, you wouldn't understand. You didn't phone just to tell me that, did you, Lieutenant?"

His voice was a little stiffer. "No, I didn't. I phoned to tell you that we're setting up a stake-out. We expect he'll be approached further by these gamblers, and we'd like to be ready for that eventuality."

"You've decided they're gamblers, have you?"

Annoyance in his voice. "What else?"

"Crackpots, Forty-niner fans, would-be humorists—"

"All right," he interrupted, "the possibility of that has been gone over very thoroughly in this office. We've decided to take no chances. But young Quirk insists that you be included in any plans of ours. He'll pay your fee.''

"He's a gentleman," I said. "I await your command, Lieutenant.''

"It's Quirk's idea, not mine," he made clear. "He wants you to move in with him. Are you currently available for full-time duty?"

"I think I can arrange it," I said thoughtfully. "When do I move in?"

"As soon as possible. And I'll want you to keep in close touch with us.''

"Of course, Lieutenant," I said respectfully. "You can always expect the fullest co-operation from this office.''

On which pleasant note we closed the conversation. And five minutes later, I'd locked the office door and was on my way home for some clothes to last me for a short stay at the Quirk home.

~~~~~~~~~~~~~~ *THREE* ~~~~~~~~~~~~~~

THE QUIRK house looked out of place in its grove of eucalyptus trees. It was a two-story mansion of red brick, a cross between Colonial and early-century Illinois. A wall of cedars hid it from view of the Sunset Boulevard traffic some two hundred yards from the front door. There it stood, a reminder of an earlier era, amidst the ultramodernity of Beverly Hills. I drove into the parking area at the side of the house and took my grip with me to the front door.

A Negro servant answered my ring. He told me, "Mr. Quirk is waiting for you in the living room, sir. He would like to talk to you."

I thought he meant Johnny, but it was the elder Quirk who was slumped in a big chair near the fireplace in the living room. It was Johnny's dad, Mr. Joseph Quirk.

He was a stocky man of medium height with a florid complexion and lustrous white hair. He looked tired and troubled.

He said quietly, "Sit down, Mr. Callahan."

I sat down and there was a silence of perhaps half a minute. Then he said wearily, "You've no children, Mr. Callahan."

I shook my head. "I'm not married, sir."

"I've two," he said. "A daughter who wants to be a movie star and a son who wants to play football. What's wrong with kids these days?"

"Since there's been football and movies, they've attracted the young ones," I said. "Johnny looked like a pretty solid kid to me. Of course, I only talked to him for an hour or so."

"He is a solid kid. I thought he had more sense than he has. He was always an intelligent boy. But is football an intelligent occupation for a *man?*"

"Some intelligent men think so."

"Coaches, you mean?"

"And professional players. Some of them have pretty high IQ's. Over 160, some of them."

"All right, all right, I'll change my question. Is it an intelligent occupation for *sensible* men?"

"I couldn't answer you objectively, sir. I played professional ball, myself."

"I know you did. But your father didn't have a number of influential friends who wanted you in their businesses, did he?"

"No, sir, he didn't. That might have made a difference to me." I knew I was lying, but is was probably what he wanted to hear.

Another silence, and then Mr. Quirk said, "I wonder if you would do me a very big favor?"

I looked at him and waited.

His voice had some pleading in it. "I wonder if you will try to discourage him in this—this trade of his?"

"How, sir?"

"Tell him what a rough and nasty business it is. That wouldn't be a lie. I've made inquiries; I know that wouldn't be a lie."

"I'd be telling him something he knew," I said. "The Rams don't all wear face masks for nothing."

"I know. But John's arrogant, though it isn't as noticeable as it once was. I didn't mean you should frighten him. I thought you could explain that the—doubtful rewards aren't quite enough pay for the punishment one takes, and the danger of permanent injury."

I didn't say anything.

Quirk's smile was resigned. "I suppose you couldn't tell him that and make it sound as though you believed it?"

"I'm afraid I couldn't, sir." I took a deep breath. "As I told Miss Curtis this afternoon, though, a man can't play professional football forever. In four to seven years, Johnny will have all of it he'll want. And a football reputation won't hurt him any in business, sir."

There was the sound of the front door closing and then

Johnny came into the room from the entry hall.

He waved at me and smiled at his dad. "Chin up, Pop. You'll be proud of me yet."

His father said, "I've been proud of you since the day you were born. Johnny doesn't drink, Mr. Callahan, but how about you?"

"Just beer," I said.

He rang for a servant and, when the maid appeared, looked at me again. "Any special kind of beer, Mr. Callahan?"

"Einlicher, if you have it, please," I said. Only among my clients do I ever find Einlicher.

The maid went out and Johnny stretched out on a twelve-foot davenport. "Hard day?" I asked him.

"We didn't practice. Just a skull session. It's been a day full of cops, though. They can be tiring."

"You're a big man," I said. "They worry about you."

"Yesterday I was a big man," he corrected me. "Next week I'm a bum again."

"I doubt it," I said. "I think you've found yourself with the Rams. It takes time to get the feel of a team, as you probably know better than I do."

"Who knows more than Brock the Rock?" he kidded me. "You should have got Pool's job."

The maid brought in my beer and Mr. Quirk rose. He said, "You gentlemen will have to excuse me. I have a number of phone calls to make before dinner."

Johnny waited until his father had left the room. Then he said quietly, "I suppose he's tried to influence you to influence me?"

I paused. "Ah—something like that." I sipped the Einlicher.

"I don't drink in front of him," Johnny said. "He's a tee-to-taler."

"If I'd known that, I wouldn't have asked for the beer."

"Oh, he doesn't mind it in others. And I suppose I could drink without breaking his heart. But I figured it was about time I thought of him a little more."

I didn't say anything. There wasn't anything very bright I could think of.

"You see," Johnny went on, "I was a real twenty-two-carat son-of-a-bitch as a kid."

"Oh?"

"In trouble with a girl when I was fifteen. The girl was much older."

"It happens to rich kids," I said.

"No, the girl was no fortune hunter. She was one of my teachers. She tried to commit suicide."

I took a deep breath. "I'm not a priest, Johnny."

He tilted his head up to grin at me. "Don't worry, I won't break down and confess all. I'm just thinking aloud. I was always too lucky; too rich, too good at sports. I was one of the most arrogant bastards in the world when I was in high school."

"And Princeton?"

"Not much better."

"And then you joined the Rams and the Deacon made a Christian out of you."

He shook his head. "They all did. You know what the sports writers were saying about me, and the sportscasters."

I nodded. "That bothered you?"

"It certainly did. But there wasn't a man on the team who wasn't rooting for me to make good."

"They expect arrogance in quarterbacks," I said. "Maybe you wouldn't have had the same tolerance as a guard."

"Maybe. And maybe I just grew up, all of a sudden. That's no place for boys, that National League, is it? That's a game for men only."

I nodded and he sat up. "Boy, I surely bent your ear, didn't I? C'mon, I'll show you your room."

The bedroom he showed me to was only about twice as big as my entire apartment in Westwood. It was in the front of the house, upstairs, and I could see most of Beverly Hills over the tops of the cedars that screened us from the road.

It had its own dressing room and its own bath. The dressing room had one wall devoted to drawers, but one drawer took care of the few shirts I had brought. I was standing by the window looking down at the richest little city in the world when the butler came to tell me dinner was about ready.

Johnny and his dad were waiting in the living room and there was a third member of the family there now and I was introduced to her.

It was Johnny's sister, Moira. She was a slim girl, fairly tall, and she looked both high-bred and high-spirited. Her hair was a dark and glowing red, her eyes some shade between gray and green.

She told me I didn't look like a policeman, as we were introduced. It was the second time I'd been told that today. I told her that it was a part of my business not to look like a policeman. That ended our living-room dialogue, but I was conscious of her appraising glances from time to time.

Over the dinner table Mr. Quirk told us about his early years in the state. He'd come here from a small town in Illinois and gone into the hardware business. From that to real estate, and I could guess it had been real estate that had made his fortune.

And where was I from, he wanted to know.

I told him I'd known only three places of residence, San Diego, Long Beach and Los Angeles.

That ended my contribution; Mr. Quirk went on to tell us some of the fabulous real-estate deals that had transpired in his lifetime. When a man dwells that consistently on the past, he is getting old in mind if not in body. Johnny was his only future.

Johnny listened politely; Moira made no effort to hide her boredom. I enjoyed the food and managed to look interested enough to keep him going.

Later, Johnny and I went for a swim in the indoor pool, and there he told me, "I hope Dad didn't bore you. He can get dull, talking about the past."

"I'm being paid by the day," I reminded him.

He smiled. "Sure. I'm going to make him proud of me yet. I gave him some bad years. I'll give him some good ones."

And then some others came; Johnny's Deborah and a lad named David Keene and some tall and elegant swain of Moira's. And a young married couple whose names I have forgotten now.

It was all very gay and young and rich and the talk was about people I didn't know and parties I hadn't attended. But that wasn't rude of them; I was here as hired help.

Both Deborah and Moira did very well by a bathing suit,

but I would still take my Jan in one of those and give them twenty-three points.

Around eleven-thirty, the others went on to one of the night spots on the Strip, but Johnny didn't go along. As we went up the stairs to the bedrooms he looked bored and weary.

"Nice gang," I said.

"They're all right. I—feel like they belong to another world." He paused. "Except for Deborah, of course."

"A lot of people would like to be in that world."

"More people would rather be Johnny Quirk yesterday."

"Only football fans. Everybody wants to be rich."

"Not me," he said. "I just want to be the best damned quarterback the Rams ever had." He stopped at the top of the stairs to face me. "Consider this—my dad's one of the wealthiest men in this state, and this is a big state. And yet, right now I'll bet you a hundred times as many people have heard of me."

The competitive urge. The thing that makes all athletes tick. But Johnny had even carried it to his dad.

I said, "Get a good night's sleep, mister. There are some brutal days ahead."

When I came into my bedroom, I didn't turn on the lights right away, because through the window I could see the lights of the city and it was such an impressive sight I wanted a good look at it.

That's how I happened to notice the car parked down at the Sunset end of the driveway. For a moment it worried me. Then the headlights of a passing car illuminated it and I saw it was a police car. The little sanctuary of Beverly Hills was taking good care of one of its most prominent citizens.

Tuesday, September sixth, I was wakened by the sun coming through the big windows. It was going to be a hot day.

In the paneled breakfast room Johnny was eating with a man I hadn't met. He was a beefy gentleman, not too tall, with a flat nose and a soft, almost womanly mouth.

He was Sergeant Gnup, of the Beverly Hills Police. He didn't look particularly ecstatic about meeting me. He told me, "I'll take over from here, Callahan. You sleep late, don't you?"

Johnny smiled and winked at me.

I said, "I'm a little new at this kind of work."

Gnup put three spoonfuls of sugar into his coffee very deliberately. He didn't look at me as he said, "This is no job for an amateur."

I couldn't think of an answer to that one and I wouldn't have voiced it if I could. I have my office in Beverly Hills. I ate in respectful silence while Johnny told Gnup his plans for the day.

Mr. Quirk came in as they were getting ready to go. He looked from Gnup to me and then at Johnny. "Isn't Mr. Callahan going with you?"

Gnup said, "Lieutenant Remington thought it would be better if we took over during the day, sir."

Quirk looked at me, waiting for a comment.

I said, "They've got the men and the experience, sir."

"All right." Quirk looked at Gnup and said quietly, "His safety will be your responsibility, then."

Gnup colored slightly and nodded.

I asked, "Shall I stay here, or does this end my participation?"

Gnup said, "We won't be home again until dinnertime. If Mr. Quirk wants you to sleep here, he'll let you know."

Quirk said flatly, "I'll want him here when John comes home."

Johnny smiled. "That should be around six o'clock. I'll see you then, Brock."

They left, and Quirk looked at me. "Did you talk to John about—about the perils of his trade?"

"Not very much, Mr. Quirk."

"You will, though, won't you?"

I paused, trying to think of the tactful answer. I was in business in this town and he was one of the leading citizens.

He said, "You've too much conscience, Mr. Callahan. That's not always an asset in business." He sat down at the table. "You needn't answer my question." He picked up the paper and ignored me.

Well, damn him. He wasn't a football fan, so how could I explain my position to him? And why should I have to explain my position to him? He had hired me as a bodyguard, not a youth counselor.

I was going through the entrance hall to the front door when Moira Quirk came down the stairs.

"Finished with the case already, Mr. Callahan?" she asked brightly.

"I'll be back this evening," I answered.

Her smile seemed superior. "We'll be waiting."

Don't hold your breath, I almost said, but didn't. Not to the Quirks of Beverly Hills.

In the parking area, the flivver waited patiently. The plastic seat was hot and the steering wheel almost untouchable. I opened the front windows and the left-hand vent and drove slowly down the long driveway to Sunset Boulevard.

My office wasn't hot; it still held the cool of the night. It's on the east side of the street. There had been a call from Jan Bonnet, my phone-answering service informed me.

I phoned her shop and her home, but there was no answer at either place. My mail consisted of one bill, two ads and a letter from my aunt in La Jolla. She wanted to know why I hadn't been up to visit her and could I get her a pair of good seats for the Detroit Lion game in October? Her latest boy friend was a Ram fan, it seemed.

I got out my books and figured my income for the year, so far, and compared it with my expenses. It would have been more profitable, I learned, for me to have gone to work at Douglas.

But of course I wouldn't meet people like the Quirks at Douglas. Though to balance that, I wouldn't meet people like Sergeant Gnup, either.

I had put the books away and was opening the *Examiner* to Vincent X. Flaherty when my door opened.

The man standing there was fairly big and rather handsome and his tailoring was far superior to mine. He smiled genially. "Mr. Callahan, I believe?"

"Right. What brings you to my humble office, Enrico Martino?"

His smile faded for only an instant. "My friends call me Rick, Rick Martin."

"I guess I'm not one of your friends. The men's room is

two doors further down the hall.''

"Why the belligerence?" he asked me calmly.

Why indeed? I said, "Sit down, Mr. Martino, and unfold your story."

"Oh, I just dropped in," he said. He came over to sit in my customer's chair. He took a package of cigarettes from the pocket of his beautiful flannel jacket and lighted one. "We— have a mutual friend, I believe. Miss Jan Bonnet?"

I nodded. "I know her."

"Excellent taste," he said. "She did my home. I live here in Beverly Hills, you know."

"I didn't know. I'll try to be more respectful."

He studied me quietly for seconds. "What's your beef with me, Callahan?"

"Nothing specific," I said, "just general. I don't like gamblers much and pimps less. Maybe I was on a clean-living kick too long. You didn't drop in to pass the time of day, did you?"

He shook his head, looking at me as dispassionately as a diner at a menu. He flicked some ash from his cigarette. "Not completely. I've been wondering about Johnny Quirk."

"What have you been wondering about him?"

"What the real story is. You know it, don't you?"

"The story of Sunday's game, you mean? You were there. You know as much about it as I do."

He shook his head. "I've been approached by the local police, Callahan. In a purely advisory way, I might add. Some gambler has threatened Quirk, hasn't he?"

"That might be."

He smiled. "That mustn't happen to one of our Beverly Hills boys, right?"

"I guess the police would figure that, if he was approached. What brought you to me?"

"I saw you leave the Quirk house a little while ago. You've been called in on the case, haven't you?"

Silence, for a few seconds. Then I said evenly, "If there was a case, and I was called in on it, I certainly wouldn't discuss it with outsiders."

No resentment in the bland face. "You can't be that rich. The pros don't pay that much to guards. You could use a friend who might have work for you from time to time."

"I certainly could," I agreed. "But if I want to stay in the honest end of this business, there are certain companions I'd better avoid. You'd be one of them. Good day to you, Enrico."

He was silent. Then he stood up and looked down at me condescendingly. "You poor, cheap slob."

"Beat it, Martino," I said. "It's been a bad morning."

He snorted in disgust. "Look, muscles, before I got smart, I spent three years as an amateur fighter. Don't try to scare me."

I stood up slowly and leaned across the desk. I reached a right hand out and slapped him sharply on the left cheek. "Run, Enrico, run for help."

I saw his right fist clench and then his left. I waited for his Latin temper to boil over. But the veneer held; Rick Martin was now a respected citizen of Beverly Hills.

He said softly, "You'll have reason to regret that, Callahan, I'm sure we'll meet again." He went out and left a quiet deep enough for me to hear the pound of my heart.

That was Tuesday, and the only other important thing that happened was a phone call from Lieutenant Remington. He told me that I wouldn't be needed at the Quirk home that night; they would take over that end, too.

I said stiffly, "Mr. Quirk hired me, Lieutenant. You didn't."

His voice sharpened. "He authorized me to tell you this. And I have. Don't be belligerent, Callahan. Men in your profession need all the police co-operation they can get."

"I've sure been getting a hell of a lot of it," I said, and hung up on him.

My phone rang again almost immediately, but I ignored it. I looked in the phone book and saw that David Keene had a bookstore not too far from here.

I walked over. One of the clerks directed me to a small office at the rear of the store, and I found David Keene there, going over a stamp album.

There was surprise on his intelligent young face. "Nothing's happened to John, has it?"

I shook my head. "You're a pretty good friend of his aren't you?"

He smiled and shrugged. "I suppose. It's only recently that he's been really friendly, though. Why do you ask?"

"You've known him a long time?"

"Since we were six. What's on your mind, Mr. Callahan?"

"Who's the girl he had out Sunday night?"

Keene frowned. "I don't know. John's probably had a lot of girl friends I don't know about."

"This must be one he was ashamed of. Is there some actress or singer he's been seeing?"

Keene smiled. "You'd better not let Moira hear you use that tone of voice when you talk about actresses."

"C'mon, David," I said impatiently. "If Johnny's got a hot number lined up, he'd tell the boys about it. He wouldn't tell his dad or Moira or Miss Curtis. But I'll bet he told you."

Keene looked at me solemnly and shook his head. "He didn't tell me whom he was with Sunday night."

"But has he talked about some girl?"

Keene nodded. "Yes. But in confidence."

I said patiently, "I have only Johnny's interests at heart. I'm no snooper."

For a moment he looked uncertain. And then he said, "There's a girl named Jackie Held he's been seeing. I suppose that's a nickname for Jacqueline. She's a TV bit player, I heard, and without any noticeable talent. *Dramatic* talent, of course, I mean."

"Do you think he had her out Sunday night?"

"I don't know. Any other questions, Mr. Callahan?"

I inclined my head toward the books in the store. "Have you read all those?"

He smiled. "More than I should have, perhaps."

"Then maybe you could tell me what 'day of the ram' means?"

He closed his eyes in thought. "Let's see—it was a Babylonian feast day. And—now, wait—" He grimaced. "It was in honor, I'm sure, of some man of great physical prowess, though I've forgotten the man, now. You see, The Babylonian calendar was divided according to reigns, and—''

"I know," I told him. "Believe it or not, I went to Stanford. And thanks a lot for the girl's name, David. I don't think you betrayed a confidence. I'm sure the police got her name from Johnny."

He nodded. "They probably did. Well, Mr. Callahan, if you should ever need a good book—''

"I'll know where to get it," I finished for him. "Thanks a lot."

Wednesday I worked on another job, a rather detailed credit and character check on a man who was courting a local heiress. The girl's papa wanted a good job done and he was willing to pay for it. Thursday morning I was still working on it. I'd found Jackie Held's address and tried to phone her intermittently through this period. But without success.

Thursday noon I had lunch with Jan. I told her about Rick Martin's visit and most of the conversation we'd had.

Jan sighed. "You couldn't be nice, I suppose?"

"Why should I be nice to a man like that?"

"Rick explained why. Because he might have use for a man in your profession from time to time. And also because Mr. Martin is a wealthy member of this community."

"Jan, I simply haven't your tolerance, I guess. Or maybe I've seen more of Mr. Martin's kind."

She looked at me suspiciously. "What did all that mean?"

I said nothing.

Her eyes were beginning to flare. "Because he's handsome, is that why you think I like him?"

I said rigidly, "That isn't why. Stop talking like that."

Her voice was softer. "All right. I'm sorry." She looked at me frowningly. "But you must learn to get along with people, Brock, all kinds of people, if you're in business. You know that, don't you?"

"Yes'm," I said. "I try to get along with them. But they don't try to get along with me."

"Well, try harder," she said.

And I agreed I would.

Thursday afternoon I continued on the case of the doubtful suitor and found enough to give my client cause for doubt. Which was probably all he wanted. I felt faintly shamed of my role as a possible romance wrecker, but the size of the fee would salve a lot of conscience.

I still hadn't been able to reach Jackie Held.

Thursday evening, around eight-thirty, I was taking a shower when my phone rang.

It was Lieutenant Remington. "I'm over at the Quirk residence. Mr. Quirk wants you to come immediately."

"Right. Has something happened, Lieutenant?"

"Something's happened. Johnny Quirk's dead. He was murdered."

∾∾∾∾∾∾∾∾∾∾∾∾∾∾∾∾ *FOUR* ∾∾∾∾∾∾∾∾∾∾∾∾∾∾∾∾

THE AMBULANCE WAS coming down the driveway as I went up it. In that ambulance was a man now dead who had known his greatest day only four days ago. I'm not unduly sentimental, but my eyes were wet when I pulled the Ford into the parking area. It was loaded with police cars.

Gnup was at the door, keeping the reporters and photographers out of the house. He looked at me bleakly and signaled me in.

I remembered the morning Mr. Quirk had told Gnup that Johnny was *his* responsibility and could guess why Quirk had asked for me.

The Negro butler led me to a study I hadn't previously seen. It was one of the wings at the end of the outdoor pool, with doors that led to the pool and the patio. It looked more like an office than a study and Joseph Quirk sat in a swivel chair behind the desk.

He was like a rock. Only his eyes moved as he considered me. "I listened to the bastards," he said hoarsely.

"What bastards, Mr. Quirk?"

"Remington and that flat-nosed idiot. They conviced me you weren't necessary to John's safety."

I said nothing. Quirk looked to me like he was holding himself together by a prodigious effort of will. I could sense that when he broke, it would be like the powdering of a rock.

Quirk's voice grew more labored. "And then Johnny conviced them that note was some kind of joke perpetrated by former teammates."

"I see, sir. He tried to give me the same story."

Quirk nodded like a robot. "But you didn't believe it, did you?"

I shook my head.

"And if he had insisted to you that it was true, what would you have done?"

"I would have checked with the players Johnny claimed were in on the hoax."

"Of course you would. And until the time you checked with them, you would have maintained your vigilance, wouldn't you?"

Honesty now? Or what he wanted to hear? I could imagine Jan holding her breath and waiting for me to say the smartly commercial thing. I said slowly, "I'm not sure. I hope I would have, sir."

"You would have. I want you to work on this, Mr. Callahan. You have a one-man office?"

I nodded.

"I want you to give it all your attention. I don't care whether you co-operate with the police or not. If they give you any hint of nonco-operation, let me know immediately. The day my son's murderer is brought to justice, I will give you a ten-thousand-dollar bonus. I don't want you to think . . ."

He paused, gasping for breath. Tears came to his eyes and saliva flecked his lips and I went to the door and found the butler quietly standing there.

"A doctor, quickly!" I said, and the man nodded and told me, "He's been standing by, sir."

He gestured, and a tall man with a doctor's bag came down the hall from the shadows at the far end.

I told the butler, "He won't need me right now. I'll talk to the police."

The butler nodded. "You never should have left Johnny, Mr. Callahan. No matter who told you to, you shouldn't have left Johnny."

I didn't answer him. I went into the big living room. Moira was talking to a uniformed man. Lieutenant Remington was just going out of the room.

And with him was Enrico Martino, now know as Rick Martin.

I crossed over to intercept them, but Remington waved me away. "I'm busy, Callahan. You can get the story from Sergeant Gnup or Officer Boldt."

Rick Martin looked at me speculatively as they went past.

Officer Boldt was the uniformed man who was talking to Moira Quirk. I went to the doorway to talk to Gnup.

Most of the reporters and photographers were piling into their cars, ready to follow Remington and Martin to Headquarters. That was the big news.

Gnup looked at me and down at the cars. "Stinking vultures."

"People like to read about it. They just supply a need."

"Brassy bastards." His soft mouth looked petulant. "They'll sure try to make me look bad."

That shouldn't be hard, I thought. But I said, "How did it happen?"

"Martino's story is that Johnny phoned him to meet him down there in that grove near the bend on Mira Road. You know, near the intersection with Sunset Boulevard. That's the end of this property."

"I know the spot. Why should Johnny phone Martino?"

"The guy claims Johnny was being bothered by gamblers and he wanted Martino to help him."

"It sounds phony to me," I said.

Sergeant Gnup spit on a nearby bougainvillaea. "And me. So the Martino parks on Sunset and starts walking over toward where he sees Johnny waiting, and—blowie—!"

I stared at Gnup blankly. "Blowie? What do you mean?"

"Young Quirk drops like he's been shot through the head. Which figures, because he was shot through the head."

"And Martin?"

"He ran right up here, he claims, and told the butler about what happened. The butler phoned us." Gnup sniffed.

"Why didn't Johnny meet Martin in the house if he wanted to talk to him?"

"You tell me," Gnup answered.

"What's Martin's story on that?"

"He says Johnny told him that he didn't want his dad to know about it."

Silence for a moment, and then I said, "So?"

"So the boys at the station will work it out of him. No

weapon on him, see, and no weapon found yet. But he could have been fingering him for somebody in a passing car, right?''

"Maybe," I said. "Though it would take some marksman to shoot a man through the head from a moving car."

"Not an approaching car, at a straightaway angle. A passing car, hell yes, but not an approaching car."

"How about the bullet? What caliber?"

"We haven't got it yet. But they'll find it. They've got a floodlight rigged up down there now and they're going over the area inch by inch."

Boldt came to the door then, and Gnup told him, "Stay here for a few minutes. I'm going down to see what the boys have found."

I went along with him to where one corner of the estate glared under the floodlights. One of the lights blinked off as we came closer, and a uniformed man saw us coming and waved us over.

The bullet had gone into a tree, and they were not attempting to dig it out. As the uniformed man explained, "It's a job for Doc Guerny. If we try to pry it out, we'll scratch it up and maybe spoil the chances for identification."

Gnup nodded. "Leave one of the lights on and send a man up to the house to phone Doc." Gnup's glance went from the road to the tree and then he went over to stand at a spot about ten feet away. He beckoned me over.

"Here's where young Quirk fell. Do you see that it's right in line with the road before the turn and that tree where the bullet is? Do you see what an easy shot it would be?"

Headlights from Sunset kept coming, holding steadily on us until they started the swing of the curve. I said, "It could be." I turned to study a small monument behind me. "What's this?"

"A grave," Gnup said.

The light was bright here and I went over to read: *Moira Quirk. Born March 3, 1901. Died September 8, 1941.*

"Johnny's mother," I said. "He told me she died when he was nine."

Gnup nodded. "And did you notice the day she died. September eighth.

I looked at him blankly and then realized that today was September eighth.''

An officer went by, rolling up the heavy-duty cable that had fed one of the lights. A breeze from the east rattled the leaves of the eucalyptus trees and a few pods fell on the grave. On Sunset, the cars slowed and then sped up again as the occupants saw there was no movie being shot under the lights.

Gnup said, ''Well, I guess we can't do any more good here. The word is that you'll be working with us, Callahan.''

''I hope to,'' I said. ''What about that girl Johnny was with Sunday night? What'd she tell you?''

''We never got her name. That kid could be stubborn.''

I started to tell him her name and then realized I didn't really know whether Jackie Held had been with Johnny Sunday night. I could always tell him later; I remained silent.

We were going up the slope to the house now. Gnup said, ''You must be in pretty solid with old man Quirk.''

''I guess so,'' I said. ''Does it bother you, Sergeant, to have to treat me like a human being?''

He said wearily, ''I can get along with anybody. But don't get the idea we're afraid of any local citizens, Callahan. The Chief can have my job any time he wants it.''

''Okay, Sergeant. Let's hope he won't want it.'' I left him at the front door and went over to my car.

A reporter and a photographer were standing next to it. ''Mr. Callahan?''

''That's right.''

''Jest, from the *Mirror*. You going to work on this?''

''I'm not sure yet.''

''Make a good story, you know, former Ram star to hunt down killer of the new Ram wizard.''

''I guess it would.''

A flash bulb went off and then the reporter said, ''You don't seem very interested. You could use the publicity, couldn't you?''

''I'm not sure,'' I told him. ''A boy has just been killed. Do you think this is the proper time for me to make hay out of that?''

Silence for a few seconds and then the photographer said,

"C'mon, Hank, you won't get anywhere with this square."

They went away and I climbed into the Ford. Johnny Quirk was dead; the significance of it was growing in me. Rich, young and about to be famous, now dead.

And why?

If Rick Martin had had anything to do with it, he wouldn't have come up to the house to report himself on the scene. And he wouldn't set up a kill where he was sure to be involved, in view of all that traffic on Sunset Boulevard. As a matter of fact, it was probably the traffic that had motivated Martin's trip to the house to report. The natural impulse for a man in his position would be to get away from the scene and set up an alibi.

Either Martin was innocent or he was imaginative and clever. I didn't think he was imaginative or clever.

I saw the butler's sad, black face again and heard the words: "You never should have left Johnny, Mr. Callahan."

More than that, I should have talked to Johnny longer that Monday he came into my office. I should have explained that I sold *privacy* and that the Ram management had enough prestige in this town to insure that privacy. He was a kid in trouble, and he had come to me. And I'd dragged him down to the cops.

There was probably a Johnny Quirk story nobody would ever know now. Young men have a tendency to regard their sins as unique and beyond understanding, to feel a shame the sins don't warrant.

I'd been heading toward the police station but I changed my course. I headed toward Pico, and an address I'd been phoning but hadn't reached. It was in West Los Angeles, within a block of the huge Twentieth Century-Fox Studios.

It was a triplex of redwood trim on gray stucco, on one level, staggered back from the quiet street in front. The rear unit was the one I'd been phoning. There was a light showing now.

It was a little short of eleven o'clock and I didn't think any citizen would relish being bothered by a private investigator that late. So when the blonde opened the door to my ring, I told her who I was and added, "I'm working with the Beverly Hills Police."

Her face should have been young, because she was, but too

much plucking and preening had made it old. Her voice was midwestern. "This isn't Beverly Hills. Why are you here, Mr. Callahan?"

"I'm investigating Johnny Quirk's whereabouts on last Sunday evening."

She studied me silently. Then she opened the door wider and I saw she was wearing a maroon flannel robe and mules. Her bleached hair was up in pins. Even the robe couldn't hide the slightly overlush breasts and hips. She was a woman designed for the bed and nothing beyond.

She nodded for me to come in, and I went into a living room crowded with too much chintzy furniture. A gas jet burned in a high hearth fireplace in one corner of the room.

"Sit down anywhere," she said.

I sat on a maple davenport with flowered upholstery. She went over to sit in a wing-back maple chair. There was some nervousness in her glance as she studied me. Then she asked, "Has something happened to Johnny? He's missing, isn't he?"

I nodded. "He was with you Sunday night, wasn't he? He told me he was, Monday morning."

"Did he? He told me not to tell anybody, and especially the police. He told me he was mixed up in trouble and he didn't want me involved in it."

"He didn't tell me as a policeman," I said. "I used to play football for the Rams, too."

Her face looked less wary. "I see." She chewed her lower lip. "Restless damned kid . . . He probably just took off on a little trip."

I shook my head. "I think it's more serious than that, Miss Held. He's a wealthy boy, you know. He might have been kidnapped. This much I know, his dad would pay *plenty* for any information that might help to bring him back."

The gas jet sputtered in the quiet room. Jacqueline Held stared at me.

I said, "When did you hear from him last?"

She picked nervously at the glazed surface of the chair's upholstery. "He phoned me yesterday, right after practice. I don't know from where. He told me he might not be over for a couple of days because the police were guarding him.''

"And Sunday night?"

"We went to the Orleans Room. Johnny's crazy for that Dixieland band. He was all worked up. I guess he had a big day at the Coliseum."

I nodded. "He tried to con me that he took you to a movie. That wasn't true, eh?"

She frowned. "Movie? Gawd, no, not for Johnny. I like 'em, being in the trade and all, and I figure a girl can always learn, you know. But Johnny—" She shook her head.

"I thought I recognized you," I lied. "I've seen you on TV, haven't I?"

She blossomed slightly. "No kidding? Big Town, maybe? I had three lines in that."

"That's it," I lied. "Just that one glimpse, and man, did you ever project. The whole screen seemed to come alive when you came on."

"That's what I've got," she agreed. "And *that's* what I've got to make them see. And I will, don't worry. Once I get an agent with—"

"I wonder why Johnny lied about the movie," I interrupted.

She stopped talking, her mouth open. Some of the light went out of her face. "Gee, I've no idea. He's kind of a—a secretive kid, you know. I can't always figure Johnny."

"Did he drink?"

"Sunday night? Not much. He never does. A couple of highballs, and he's had it."

"How about the note that was left in his car?" I asked.

"Note?" She stared at me blankly. "What note?"

"He told me he found a typewritten note in his car. He showed it to me in my office."

Her face was as thoughtful as its artificiality permitted. And then she nodded. "I remember he picked something off the seat. I asked him what it was, and he told me it was just an advertisement folder, probably. But he put it in his jacket pocket, I remember."

"He didn't read it before he put in into his pocket?"

She shook her head. "I don't think so. It wasn't light enough, and he didn't look at it long. What'd the note say?''

"It wasn't clear to us. Johnny may know what it meant. We think it was from some gamblers.''

She stared. "A—a threat?''

"No, not exactly. An offer to do business. Have you had much experience with gamblers, Miss Held?''

She started to answer, and then she stopped and the wariness was back in her face. "What do you mean by that, mister?''

"Do you know any?''

"What if I do?''

"We'd be interested. You can tell me about it here, in the privacy of your home, or you can get dressed and come over to the station and tell it to some less sympathetic officers.''

Her face was flintlike. "Some change in you, Mr. Callahan. I'll get dressed. And then I'll phone my lawyer and we'll go down to the station. Is that all right?''

"That's all right with me if that's the way you want it.''

She stood up and started toward another room, when her doorbell chimed. She looked at me and at the door and she looked less frightened than nervous.

"Shall I go?'' I asked.

She shook her head impatiently and went past me. I stood up as she opened the door. I heard a man ask, "Miss Jacqueline Held?''

She nodded.

"I'm Sergeant Pascal from the West Los Angeles station. And this is Sergeant Gnup from Beverly Hills.''

I looked around for a place to hide.

"Come right in,'' Jackie Held said. "Mr. Callahan is here, too.''

ssssssssssssssssss FIVE ssssssssssssssss

I HEARD AN exclamation from Gnup and a grunt from Pascal and then both of them were in the room and facing me.

"Co-operation, huh?" Gnup said acidly. "You conniving son-of-a—"

Pascal said, "Easy, Sergeant. There's a lady present." The dour, bloodhound face of Sergeant Pascal looked almost happy. "Now we've got Golden Boy in trouble in his *own* town."

Jackie said, "If you gentlemen will excuse me for a moment, I'd like to phone my attorney."

"Hold it a minute, Miss Held. We have some questions first." Pascal looked at me. "Sit down."

I sat down.

Pascal looked at Jackie and nodded toward me. "How long have you known him?"

"I never saw him before about twenty minutes ago."

Gnup glared at me. "Co-operation, huh?"

"It's a two-way street, Sergeant," I said. "You told me tonight you couldn't get Miss Held's name out of Johnny. And now here you are."

Gnup said, "I didn't get it out of Johnny. We got it out of Martino about a half an hour ago."

"Rick?" Jackie asked quickly. "Rick gave you my name? Well, then it's all right." She turned to me. "That's the gambler I know."

Pascal said, "What did Callahan want from you, Miss Held?"

"He was questioning me about Johnny. He wanted to know about Sunday night and when I last heard from Johnny. Has Johnny been found?"

"Found?" Gnup said. Both men looked at her blankly.

"Mr. Callahan said he was missing, maybe kidnapped. Was that a lie?"

Both of them looked at me quietly.

I said, "Miss Held, just before the doorbell rang, where were we going?"

She frowned. "Down to the station. I suppose you meant the Beverly Hills station. That's where you're from, isn't it?"

I nodded. "And what were you going to do first?"

"I was going to phone my lawyer. You said I could."

"That's right, Miss Held." I stood up and faced the pair of sergeants. "Now, am I in trouble?"

Gnup looked doubtful. But Pascal said, "With me you are. Maybe you better phone *your* lawyer."

"All right," I said reasonably, and started for the phone.

Gnup said, "Hold it, Callahan. There'll be time for that." He looked at Jackie. "We'd like some information from you, Miss Held."

"You can get it from my attorney," she said. "Or from Mr. Callahan. I've told him everything I know."

I couldn't help the smirk and I couldn't help Pascal's seeing it. His glance was murderous. He looked back at Miss Held. "Did Callahan claim to be a police officer?"

She shook her head slowly. "Not exactly. I got the idea he was a private detective working with the Beverly Hills Police Department."

Pascal looked at Gnup questioningly.

Gnup shrugged. "I guess."

I said, "Jackie, these two men are here to search for some facts. They mean you no harm if you're not involved in what happened to Johnny. If you're clean, your most intelligent decision would be to tell them everything you know, right here and now."

She looked between us helplessly and her voice quavered. "First maybe you boys had better tell me what *did* happen to Johnny."

"He was killed," Gnup said. "He was murdered, tonight."

It was the damnedest thing. That phony, hard, theatrical face seemed to come apart, to grow soft and hold for a few moments a mask of almost classic tragedy. And then she went down, blubbering.

• • •

Ten minutes later, Pascal had bathed her face with cold water and he and Gnup were questioning her. I went out to my car. I'd heard enough to know she had told all she could.

A block away the after-theater traffic moved along Pico, but on this side of the street only the two police cars in front disturbed the night's placidity. A clear night, getting cold.

Where now? Two police departments in on the kill, with all the men and equipment and experience that meant. Where would Brock Callahan, a bumbling semipro, go to find the truth?

I felt weary and futile; I went home. Men die every minute and leave very little record of their earthly existence. Johnny had died before the records could be written. And he would have hung up some records.

Records are just ink in dusty books, but who leaves more than that behind? Kids, a man could leave some kids, but Johnny hadn't had time for that, either.

A hot shower and a can of High Life, but no peace. I tossed and turned and fretted and tried to see a pattern in the little knowledge I had garnered.

I don't remember sleeping but I must have dozed from time to time. I got up at seven and my bad knee ached. Outside, it was gray and damp.

Somebody had described Los Angeles as a dozen shopping centers in search of a town. It isn't quite that. Areas have names of their own out here, but Hollywood is still in Los Angeles and so is Westwood. And so are Brentwood and Bel-Air. But not Beverly Hills or Culver City or Santa Monica; they are distinct and separate municipalities, islands surrounded by the creeping fungus that calls itself Los Angeles.

Johnny had been a roving lad, and it was likely there would be more than one police department involved in the search for his killer. None of the department men would be likely to relish the assistance of Brock Callahan.

The *Times* had more of a story than I had learned last night. Johnny Quirk had been shot with a rifle. From a passing car, the theory was. Rick Martin had been released after questioning. The police were picking up gamblers like oranges at harvest and no lead was being overlooked. Remington's name was given more prominence than a Bullock's department store ad but there was no mention of Brock (the Rock) Callahan. I thought of the *Mirror* reporter last night.

I'd made the coffee too strong and there wasn't quite enough milk to soak my cornflakes properly. I read on.

Remington must have stock in the *Times;* there was not a word about the police guard on Johnny that had been relaxed too soon. There was a hint that perhaps "Rick Martin (Enrico Martino)" had been framed by rival gamblers. Or perhaps the shot had been meant for him and Johnny had died by mistake.

There were a lot of theories but there was very little substance.

There was a stone-cold lad, though, in Beverly Hills mortuary, and *somebody* had killed him. By accident or design, in malice or greed, in hate or carelessness.

I shaved and dressed and phoned the Quirk home. I asked the butler. "How is Mr. Quirk holding up?"

"He's resting, sir, under a sedative. Miss Moira is awake but taking it very hard."

"I see. I won't bother her. When is the funeral?"

"I think on Saturday, sir. It hasn't been finally determined."

I thanked him and hung up. I put some liniment on my right knee and went down to the office.

Sid Gillman, the new Ram coach, had refused to comment on what the death of Johnny Quirk would mean to the Rams' season. Sid had been the best college coach in America before taking the job with the Rams; it was obvious this morning that we not only had a great coach, we had a great gentleman.

Sid had been under fire for sticking to Johnny as long as he had; a lesser man would have made recriminatory ammunition of the bathos the sports writers were indulging in this morning.

Sports writers assume their readers have no memories. And very little sense.

There was a rumor that Dutch Van Brocklin would come out of retirement. Everybody was overlooking Dom Ristucci, it seemed.

Everybody but Flaherty. Vincent X. wrote: *This puts the temporary load on Johnny's understudy, Dom Ristucci. I think the lad will come through, though I'm sure it's a minority opinion. But then, at Notre Dame, the Midwest scribes didn't think much of Dom, at first, either. The Fresno Flash has fooled the experts before; I'm making book that he'll meet this new challenge.*

Dominic Peter Ristucci, son of an immigrant Italian grape grower in Fresno, was stepping into the vacated shoes of John Gallegher Quirk, son of a Beverly Hills millionaire. And of all the sports writers in the two papers I had read this morning, only Vincent X. Flaherty thought the shoes would fit.

A purple foot was taking over the job of a lad born to the purple, I thought. I liked that, and I rolled it over in my mind, and wondered if I wouldn't have made a good sports writer. I decided to mail it in to Vincent X.

I was imagining all the offers I would get from the various talent-hungry sports editors and I was turning them all down with high disdain when my phone rang.

It was Jan. "I've just read about that Quirk boy. Is that where you were last night, Brock?"

"That's where I was. Why?"

"We had a sort of half-date, you might remember."

Last night had been Thursday night and we usually saw each other on Thursday nights. "I'm sorry. I should have phoned." I told her.

"It doesn't matter. Isn't it horrible, Brock? Isn't it sickening?"

"Yes."

"Have the police any idea who did it? Have you?"

"I haven't. I doubt if the police have."

"And that business about Rick Martin being there, that must have seemed very suspicious to the police."

"Too suspicious to be true."

"I suppose. But I mean with Rick related to that—that Pistachio, or whatever his name is, it must certainly be the most ridiculous coincidence that—"

"Slow down," I interrupted. "I'm not following you. Who do you mean by Pistachio?"

"You know, the Quirk boy's substitute? I can never remember his name."

"Do you mean Dom Ristucci?"

"That's it. Rick told me one time that he's related to the boy. He seemed very proud of that."

"Are you sure? There was nothing in the papers about that."

"I'm sure he told me. And I remember he also told me not to mention it, because he didn't want to hurt the boy's chances. What do you think he meant by that?"

"The National Football League takes a very dim view of gamblers, Jan. That's what Enrico meant."

Silence for a second. "He really is a gambler, then? A professional gambler?"

"That's right. And before that he was tied up with white slavery. Did you think I was lying to you Sunday?"

A longer silence. "I—guess. At least I thought you were exaggerating and—being vulgar. You do both of those things quite often, Brock."

"All right, all right," I said impatiently. And then I saw my door open and in a second I saw the man standing there.

I said to Jan, "I have to hang up now. Your friend just walked in."

"What friend?"

"Enrico Martino," I said, and hung up.

He wasn't smiling this morning. Nor did he look arrogant. He looked like a worried businessman in to see his banker.

"Miss Bonnet?" he asked me, nodding toward the phone.

"That's right. Sit down, Mr. Martin."

He looked at me speculatively. "If you intend to go physical on me again, maybe we could run over to my gym for a couple rounds."

I shook my head. "Tuesday was a bad day. I apologize. If you'll apologize for calling me a poor, cheap slob."

He came over to sit in my customer's chair. "I'll take back the 'cheap' and the 'slob.' I guess you're poor enough, though, aren't you?"

"I guess. So, now?"

"Miss Bonnet told you what I was stupid enough to tell her, one time?"

"About Dom Ristucci?" I nodded. "How close is the relationship?"

"My mother was his father's cousin. That was enough for me. I don't have too much to brag about along those lines."

"The reporters will find it out eventually," I said. "It sure adds another coincidence to the bundle, though, doesn't it?"

He looked at me curiously. "Add 'em up for me. I see your in with the police and the Quirk family. Add up the case against me, as far as you have it."

"All right. You and Johnny lusted after the same girl, maybe, Jackie Held."

Martin nodded. "I'll give you more; I was paying her rent."

"That's one. You're on the scene when Johnny dies, that's two. Johnny got a note from gamblers and you're a gambler, that's three. Ristucci is your second cousin, that's four. Hell, man, I'm surprised you're walking around outside."

His smile was bleak. "Damned strange bunch of coincidences, isn't it? And there are only two possible answers, aren't there?"

I nodded.

"If you agree, what are they?" he asked me.

"Either you're guilty, or you've been jobbed."

He nodded and his eyes held mine. "Which theory do you favor, Callahan?"

I returned his gaze like the heavy in a B picture. "I couldn't honestly say, Enrico."

"Rick, huh? Rick."

"Rick."

He considered me impersonally. "You still hate my guts, don't you?"

"The life you've led, maybe. Not you, I suppose. Why did you come to see me, Rick?"

"I want you to find out who tried to frame me. I could give you some leads."

"One thing we overlooked. Johnny phoned you, didn't he? Your enemies wouldn't be likely to know that, would they?"

"How do we know it was Johnny? I didn't know the kid's voice."

"I see." I fiddled with a pencil on my desk. "I've got a job, right now. I couldn't work for two clients at the same time." I looked up at him. "Not on the same job."

"You're working for the Quirks, huh?"

I nodded.

"Regular day-to-day deal?"

"And a bonus if I find out who killed Johnny."

"How much of a bonus?"

"Ten thousand dollars."

He took out a cigarette and lighted it, trying for the casual touch. Some ham in this bum. He said lightly, "I'll match it, when you find the killer. And if I give you some leads, it might help to solve it. What can you lose?"

"What if I prove that you're the killer, Rick?"

He stood up. "Then I'll give you *twenty* thousand dollars and this arm." He made a gesture of sawing his right arm off at the shoulder. "And I'd put that in writing and have it notarized."

I smiled. "This is important to you, isn't it?"

"Very. I've got a daughter going to high school in this town."

I said nothing.

"Do you think I'd change my name otherwise? I'm not ashamed of my name."

"Assuming it was Johnny who phoned you, did he tell you he'd been contacted by gamblers?"

Martin nodded. "He said he was in a lot of trouble and he'd heard about me from Jackie Held and that she'd recommended me as a man to be trusted."

"Did Jackie admit that?"

"No, but she's not the most honest girl in the world. And if it was true, this Quirk never told the law that. Of course, Jackie told me he was a secretive kid."

"He didn't give the law her name, and they must have put on plenty of heat." I stood up and stretched my neck. "Didn't you resent Jackie messing around with this kid?"

Martin smiled and spread both hands out expansively. "I'm getting what I'm paying for. I didn't buy the girl; I was just renting her."

I shook my head. "Are you going to continue to rent her?"

"Why not? I've got a couple more like her, if you're ever in the mood."

"No, thanks." I went to the window. "I don't want your money, Rick. But who are the men?"

He handed me a plain white filing card on which two names and addresses were typed. "This isn't for the police, you know, Callahan. Not unless you get your case."

"I know." I said. "And it will probably put me in the soup.

But I've learned I have to work any way I can. I'm surprised a solid citizen like you should hate the law.''

''I'll never be respectable enough to like cops,'' he said. ''Do we shake hands or something?''

I shook his hand and was glad there were no photographers present. He went out smiling.

A couple of days ago I'd been moaning about business. Now I had more clients than I could accept.

I looked at the names on the card. One was a man I had met once and whose name was constantly in print. He had a piece of many local fighters, I'd heard, and the big piece of the state's leading welterweight.

Boxing is controlled by hoodlums in Los Angeles, as it is in most of America's major cities. But so far as I knew this man had no police record. Of convictions, at least.

I imagined my best bet with him would be to go to him openly. At first, anyway.

He lived in Brentwood, in one of the estates fronting on San Vicente. His name was Ned Allen.

I found him in the back yard, where he was putting on a sloping green. The green was better maintained than any of those on the public courses around town. I don't know about the private courses.

He was a big man, gone slightly soft, and he had gray hair, a deep tan and very nice white teeth. I saw the teeth when I introduced myself; he smiled cordially.

''I've seen you play,'' he told me. ''Aren't you a detective or something now?''

I nodded. ''I've an investigation service in Beverly Hills. I'm working with the Beverly Hills police on Johnny Quirk's death.''

His face was grave. ''Horrible thing.'' He frowned. ''But what brought you here, Mr. Callahan?''

''The possibility of gamblers being involved,'' I said frankly. ''You must know most of them, and I thought you might have heard something. And as one of our solider citizens, I guessed you'd be glad to tell the police anything you'd heard.''

He smiled wryly and stroked a ball toward one of the holes at the far end of the green. ''Start over, Mr. Callahan.''

''I don't follow you, Mr. Allen.''

"Sure you do." He stroked another ball, watched it all the way to where it stopped short of the hole and then looked at me. "I've met some mobsters from time to time. I don't associate with them. I run a clean stable, Mr. Callahan."

"I know that," I lied, "or I wouldn't be here. Wouldn't you hate to see football follow boxing's trail, sir?"

"There are honest men in boxing. Maybe not many in Los Angeles, but San Francisco's a clean boxing town. I schedule the important fights there." He walked over to retrieve the balls.

I walked along. "Perhaps you could give me a lead, sir, to somebody who could help me."

He smiled. "The man you're working for should give you plenty of leads. He probably gave you my name."

I waited until he had lined the balls up before asking, "What man, Mr. Allen?"

"A man from your town, a Beverly Hills hood named Rick Martin."

"I'm not working for Rick Martin," I said.

"Maybe not. He gave you my name, though, didn't he?"

I didn't answer. He putted a couple of balls toward a hole in the center of the sloping green. The second one dropped. He looked at me.

"Sorry to intrude," I said, and started toward the walk.

"Just a second," he said.

I stopped and turned around.

"Only because you're Brock Callahan," he said, "and, remember, *I* never told you this. But there's a man in this town who hates Martin more than I do. And for different reasons."

I waited.

"I hate Martin because he's a crook," Allen said. "This man is just a rival crook. His name is Lenny Heffner. Know him?"

"I've heard of him." It was the other name on the card. "Why does he hate Martin?"

"It started over a girl. Martin was always too lucky with other men's girls. Go easy with Heffner, though; he's even bigger than you are." He tapped another ball. "And considerably meaner." The ball dropped with a rattle.

Hams, hams, hams, this area is full of hams. The morning's

gray was lifting and I could see the dark blue edge of the Santa Monica Mountains against the clear sky.

Ned Allen had said "this town," but that's just a phrase. He meant the Los Angeles area—all of the towns roughly identified as "this town" of Los Angeles. It's really not a town at all, but a collection of attitudes.

Lenny Heffner had a small gym and bar in the crummy part of Santa Monica, right off Olympic. I didn't think he could be much, with a dive like that, but a lot of important men like to stay in their old neighborhoods.

I went into the bar and ordered a bottle of High Life. The bartender wore a clean white T-shirt and Balboa blues and blue suède shoes with crepe soles. He didn't have any Miller High Life, he told me. I ordered Budweiser.

He was a fairly young man, with brown eyes and with his dark hair in a crew cut. His skin was olive and healthy looking. He moved with the slight shoulder swagger of a boxer.

I asked, "Haven't I seen you somewhere?"

"At the Olympic, or Ocean Park." He tried to make his smile modest. "Manny Cardez."

A welterweight, a prelim boy. I'd never seen him fight but had probably seen his picture in the papers or on a poster.

"Oh, yes," I said. "How's the career going?"

"It was going all right until I met Jordan." He shrugged. "There are other ways of making a living."

"You've quit?"

"Not exactly. I keep in shape, and I can always fill in a card. It's money. I don't figure it's my career any more."

I smiled. "This is easier, eh?"

He paused a moment and glanced at me curiously. Then he shrugged again. "It's steady." Another pause. "You a salesman?"

I met his gaze. "Why?"

"Been a lot of cops around the last couple of days. And too many this morning. You're big enough to be a cop."

"This morning I can figure," I told him. "But what about the other days?"

"Some gamblers hang out here. And the cops have been checking all the gamblers in the county since Monday."

"I know," I said. "I couldn't lay a bet with my regular boy. The heat's on, I suppose, because of Johnny Quirk."

His open face was more guarded. "I suppose." He went down to the end of the bar and picked up a *Racing Form*. He gave it his attention.

From Olympic I heard the blat of a diesel making the slight climb from the tunnel that led to the Coast Highway. There was a door with a frosted-glass window in the rear wall. The washroom doors were in the wall opposite the bar.

I looked at the menu in the middle of the back-bar mirror and asked, "How are the enchiladas?"

He looked up from his *Form*. "All right. Want some?"

I nodded. "You're a welterweight, aren't you?"

He nodded. "Coffee, milk?"

"I like 'em with beer," I said.

He went up a narrow hallway at the end of the bar. He had evidently decided not to be sociable. I could sit here, I suppose, like Alan Ladd, giving the place my cold-eyed stare and waiting for some varmint to draw.

Only there weren't any varmints in sight. Just a clean and bare barroom, looking slightly old-fashioned with its scrubbed wooden floor, making the gaudy juke box seem out of place. And the clean young Spanish-American in Balboa blues didn't seem to be hunting trouble.

He brought the enchiladas and silverware and a paper napkin and went back to his reading.

No short-order slob had made these; they were delicious. I said, "I'll bet you've got a female cook."

He looked up and smiled briefly. "My aunt. More beer?"

"Please," I said. "And another order of these. I'm a big boy."

He measured me with his eyes and smiled and went up the narrow corridor again. I was finishing what was left of the first bottle of beer when the door opened.

I glanced over in my casual way and saw a girl standing in the open doorway.

It was Jackie Held.

================================ *SIX* ================================

SHE WORE A black jersey skirt with a white blouse and a short jersey jacket over the blouse. Her young-old face wore a look of consternation as she hesitated in the doorway staring at me.

"Come on in, Jackie," I said cordially. "They have the best enchiladas I've ever eaten."

Some composure came back to her artificial face. "I know. That's why I stopped. I was just driving by, and . . ."

"Me too," I said, "on the way to the beach. Don't apologize; I'm not a snob."

Her painfully plucked eyebrows lifted. "I *wasn't* apologizing, Mr. Callahan. And if I'd known you were here I wouldn't have dropped in."

I smiled at her. "Let's be friends. We'll eat together, and I won't even tell Rick I saw you here."

She glared at me. But she came over to take the stool next to mine. "Why should you tell Rick Martin anything?"

Manny Cardez was back with another plate of enchiladas. He paused at the end of the hallway when he saw Jackie. His glance shifted between us and then he came the rest of the way, his face carefully blank.

Jackie said, "I'll have some of those. And some beer, too. Einlicher, please."

There wasn't a public bar in town that had Einlicher. But Manny brought out a bottle. I said, "Make my second bottle that, too."

"It's seventy-five cents a bottle," he told me.

I smiled at him. "I can handle it. I'm on an expense account."

Plainly enough for all to hear, Jackie said, "I didn't know detectives had expense accounts."

57

"I'll bet you didn't," I answered. "And I'll bet Manny here didn't know I was a detective until this second."

The bartenders face showed nothing. He put the opened bottle of beer on the bar and went back to the hallway.

"You fixed me real good," I said. "I'll have to tell Sergeant Pascal how co-operative you've been."

Her face was rigid. "I didn't know you were—snooping. I didn't mean anything wrong."

"Uh-huh. Does Rick Martin know you hang around here?"

"I don't hang around here. And why should it be Rick Martin's business if I did?"

I didn't answer. I went to work on my second plate of hot enchiladas and ice-cold lettuce. She sipped her beer and lighted a cigarette nervously. Overhead, a plane droned, heading for the Santa Monica Airport.

Manny brought another plate of enchiladas and Jackie put out her cigarette. The bartender went over and opened the door with the frosted-glass panel. He went through it and closed it quietly behind him.

Jackie said, "Are you going to tell Rick?"

"What difference does it make?"

"All right, damn you, it makes a difference. Are you going to?"

"I don't know. Anything you want to tell me?"

She went after her enchiladas hungrily. "I suppose you think I'm some kind of—of spy or something for Lenny Heffner."

"Are you?"

"Of course not. He knows a producer I'm trying to get to, that's all."

"I see. And you came over to make a personal appeal. You've been here before, haven't you?"

"Once. With Johnny Quirk. That's when I learned they had Einlicher."

"Oh? And when did you learn Lenny Heffner knew a producer?"

"That same night. A lot of big wheels eat here. They have the best Mexican food for miles."

"Johnny knew Lenny pretty well, did he?"

"I don't know. I don't think so."

I sat there silently a moment, sipping the finest beer money can buy.

Jackie said, "There were a lot of things about Johnny people didn't know, I'll bet. He was—secretive, moody at times. You'd think he was in another world."

He was, now. I asked, "Going to the funeral?"

She shook her head emphatically. "I can't stand funerals. I couldn't even go to my dad's."

Another silence, except for the throb of traffic from Olympic. Then the glass-paneled door opened and two men came through it. They walked over without smiling.

One was big, with a bald head and light blue eyes. He looked a little soft. The other was equally big, and was dressed in a T-shirt and cocoa-brown gabardine slacks. He had curly black hair on his head and forearms and peeking out of the top of his T-shirt. He didn't look soft.

The bald one said, "Brock Callahan, right?"

I nodded.

"I'm Lenny Heffner. Cops I got to talk to; it's the law. But not you. What are you snooping around here for?"

"Einlicher and enchiladas," I answered. "What else?"

"Don't get smart," he said.

I studied both of them. "I won't if you won't. What's your beef with me, Mr. Heffner?"

"I don't want you in here."

"It's a public place. But I won't make an issue of it. When I've finished my beer, I'll go."

Curly came into the act now. He pointed a thumb at the door. "Move, Irish."

Jackie said quickly, "There's no need to get all excited, Mr. Heffner. Mr.—"

"Shut up," Heffner said.

I stepped off the stool, the bottle in my hand. I said, "I'm going to report this." I had lifted the bottle up, to sip it, when Curly reached a hand toward my shoulder. It was his left hand and his right hand was balled.

I backhanded the bottle into the side of his jaw. I heard

Jackie squeal and then something crushed my solar plexus and I went down next to the stool. Curly had swung a left hand faster than the eye.

I was sick and dizzy, but my groping hand found one leg of my bar stool and I came up swinging it. It caught Curly in the hip and he yelped, and came in before I could swing it back.

It was my lucky day. He got tangled in the rungs as I retreated and he started to fall. And I put all of my two hundred and twenty pounds into the right hand I threw at his exposed chin.

A knuckle went, and I prayed he wouldn't get up. He didn't look like a man I could handle with my left hand. He didn't get up.

I looked at Heffner. "You next?"

He didn't seem frightened. He said, "Get out. Your beer and food is on the house. But beat it."

"All right. And I'm reporting it, too. You'd be smarter to play along with me, Heffner. The whole town's behind me."

He said nothing, staring at me with those ice-blue eyes. At the bar, Jackie was sniffling. Manny Cardez came quietly through the doorway at the rear and went over behind the bar. He kept his head down, rearranging bottles.

I stared at Heffner and he stared at me, and then I turned and went out to my car. I didn't drive away immediately. I sat in the front seat, gingerly rubbing my swelling hand and watching the entrance to the bar through my rear window.

Twenty minutes went by and Jackie still hadn't come out. Maybe she was having a second helping. I considered driving over to the Santa Monica Headquarters, but decided against it.

I wondered who the curly-haired boy was and whether I'd see him again. I had a feeling he could take me any time he wanted to; that stool had been the difference today. And the hardness of that beer bottle.

But there was no point in running myself down too much; that had still been a very fine right hand.

My ribs were sore and my hand ached in a steady beat as I drove back to Beverly Hills. The morning haze had vanished completely; visibility was unlimited.

Ned Allen had told me the trouble between Martin and Heffner had started over a girl. I wondered if Jackie Held had been that girl. She was certainly moving through this case like an interlocking thread, friendly to three men. Or at least to two of them, and knowing the third.

I wondered if she was playing both ends against the middle. A girl like her would be in a position to hear things worth money. She knew men in their most intimate moments, as they say. She knew them drunk and she knew them sober. And maybe a naïve kid would tell her things he shouldn't.

But had Johnny Quirk been a naïve kid?

If he had been, and had told her things, she'd find a way to earn a dollar from them if they were salable. She worked in a hard world, a world of angles and opportunists and extremely muddy ethics. But she didn't have the muscles or the friends to play it cute with Heffner and Martin.

I went back to the office and soaked my hand. I took off my shirt and saw the red line along the ends of my ribs. Curly could have been a pro, and if he was, that was a felony. A fighter's fists are a lethal weapon in this state.

I typed up the morning's interviews, trying to recapture the phraseology as exactly as I could remember it. I included the things Rick Martin had told me and I tried to include my thoughts on all I'd learned. I had no thoughts beyond the obvious and the obvious was the same as it had been when Martin had walked in this morning.

Either he was guilty, or he'd been set up by somebody who wanted him to appear guilty. But he wouldn't have shot Johnny in plain view of all that traffic. And where was the weapon, if he had?

Had there been an accomplice in a car who had taken the weapon from him before he'd gone up to report to the house? Again, there was the traffic; somebody would have seen that. No, if Martin had killed Johnny, it hadn't been premeditated.

And *if* Johnny had phoned him, *why* had he phoned him? A number of people had called him a secretive lad; I wondered how many of his secrets had died with him.

I put what I'd typed into a folder and walked over to David Keene's bookstore. Keene was in the front of the store, staring out through the plate-glass window. He looked pale and distraught.

"I was just going out to lunch," he told me. "Have you had yours?"

I nodded. "But I could drink a cup of coffee. I'd like to talk about Johnny, if you don't mind."

He took a deep breath. "Anything that will help. I just can't—seem to accept what I know is a fact."

"He was pretty close to you, was he?"

Keene didn't answer right away. He gave it some thought. Then, "I'm not sure he was ever close to anybody, anybody male. With women, now . . ." He shrugged.

"Let's go and have lunch," I said, "and you can tell me about the women."

We ate at Leslie's while he told me some of the romantic history of Johnny Quirk. The lad had been either an awesome stud or a pathological braggart.

I said, "He was lucky, too, wasn't he? I mean, most girls are attracted to money, but the girls Johnny knew already had money."

He nodded. "The majority of them did."

I said, "I think he felt sorry for the bad time he had given his dad. How did they get along?"

"Not very well, when Johnny was younger. He might have had an Oedipus complex."

"In love with his mother, you mean?"

He nodded. "And a hatred for his father."

"But Johnny's mother died when he was nine."

"He could be in love with her memory, maybe. I don't know; I'm no psychiatrist."

"How about this teacher that he got in trouble with in high school?"

David Keene stared at me blankly. "Teacher?"

I nodded. "Johnny told me about it. Some woman he got involved with. I guess it broke her up more than it did him. And really hurt his dad."

Keene shook his head wonderingly. "That's a new one on me. You'd think I'd know about it; I went all through high school with him."

Which was true enough. But it was beginning to appear that

John Gallegher Quirk's secretiveness had many facets. There was a good chance that women had been more frequent recipients of his confidence than men had. But not the females he'd grown up with; they might be too refined to relish the real Quirk story.

I asked young Keene, "Did Johnny tell you much about this Jackie Held? Was that a major romance with him?

He looked at me candidly. "I wouldn't think so. He'd known too many show girls. But who can tell? Is she enough older so that she'd have a—a maternal appeal for him?"

I shook my head. "I doubt if she's any older than Johnny was. But she's been on her own longer, probably." I finished my coffee. "Well, there might be something there I'll never dig out. She's a pretty sly operator."

I was getting steadily nowhere. I had the feeling of a lightweight halfback beating his brains out against the Bears' line. I'd been constantly on the move since last night, but it wasn't getting me anywhere. I left David Keene at the restaurant and went back to the office. I picked up a *Herald-Express* on the way, to see if there was anything new the police hadn't kept me informed about.

The story on Dom Ristucci had come out, as I'd expected it would. His relationship to Rick Martin was termed "interesting" by Lieutenant Remington, and I could almost read the overtone of suspicion in the word.

Coach Sid Gillman of the Rams called it an "unfortunate coincidence." Which was what it looked like to me. But then I was a Ram, too. Mr. Gillman hadn't commented beyond that except to state that Dom Ristucci would be his starting quarterback in Sunday's exhibition with the Philadelphia Eagles.

I thought about the situation and realized that a fan with an overactive imagination could read a lot beyond coincidence in the setup. If the gamblers wanted to take over football as they had boxing, what better way than to kill off a man beyond price? And find as his substitute a man related to one of them.

As I've explained before, as the quarterback goes, so goes the T-formation; he's the key to success in the National Football League.

I wrote up all that David Keene had told me and phoned the Quirk residence.

The butler told me, "Mr. Quirk is under a sedative again, Mr. Callahan. Is there some way I can be of service?"

"I wondered if he wanted daily reports."

"I doubt it, sir. Results are what Mr. Quirk wants. The funeral will be tomorrow morning, sir. From Elysian Fields."

Tomorrow they would put him away. And the day after that, Dom Ristucci would trot out with the rest of the boys and the game would be on. The fans would undoubtedly think of Johnny Quirk when Dom took over the team this Sunday. But there were a lot of Sundays in a season and the name of Quirk would get dimmer every week.

There was some nausea in me; I went to the water cooler and drank a paper cup of water slowly. The sun burned through the windows to the west, but didn't warm me.

I went to the phone and called Jan.

"How are you?" I asked her.

"Not busy and a little blue. How are you?"

"Cold. Couldn't I buy some steaks for dinner and you could broil them?"

A few seconds silence. Then, "I suppose."

"I don't want to be alone tonight," I said. "I don't want to go home."

"All right," she said. "But is it love or loneliness, Brock?"

"I don't know for sure. Both, I suppose."

"I'll see you," she said.

# SEVEN

HER BEDROOM HELD a faint smell of spice. One finger traced a pattern on my chest. She said softly, "You're a fine, strong and gentle man, Brock the Rock."

"I aim to please, ma'am. You're a fine cook."

"Is that all?"

"Huh. That's all in the kitchen. You're fine all around the house, in every room."

"What were you thinking of when you phoned me?"

"Of you."

"And what else?"

"Of Johnny Quirk and the shortness of life and the coldness of the ground."

"Who wants to live forever?"

"Everybody. Almost everybody."

"Not I," she said. "Do you want to sleep now? *Can* you sleep now?"

"I can sleep now," I said.

The last sound I remember was a bark from the Doberman next door. He hates me and loves Jan. Maybe he's jealous.

I dreamed of a putting green atop a tall building and a ball that went over the edge and I remember leaning over the edge of the building to watch the ball fall toward the toy cars and people below.

I wakened to a sunny room and the sound of a power lawn mower next door. My right hand was stiff and the soreness in my ribs was still present.

When I came out to the kitchen, later, Jan was whipping up some eggs and cream in a huge yellow bowl.

"Omelet and pork sausages," she told me. "Good enough?"

"Excellent. Anything I can do?"

"Relax. Pretend you're a husband."

I looked at her face to see if there was any meaning in that, but saw no bitterness. "You make more money than I do," I said.

She looked up quickly, puzzled. Then she smiled.

"Oh. I meant nothing, lover. Don't sound so—trapped."

The *Times* was on the coffee table in the living room; I brought it out to the kitchen.

A sports reporter I'd rather not name devoted his column to the relationship between Dom Ristucci and Enrico Martino. The hack tried to be subtle about it, but subtlety was beyond his talent. He was an ignorant blusterer and the piece couldn't have been much more than an inch short of libel.

Jan asked, "What are you muttering about now?"

"Nothing. The funeral's this morning, Johnny Quirk's funeral. I'm going to it."

"I'm not. I can't stand funerals." She was at the stove and staring unseeingly at the griddle when she asked, "Brock, do you have—any other girls?"

"None. But you have other men."

"Dates, yes."

I looked at her until she turned to face me. Then I said, "So?"

"So we're kind of moral, aren't we? That's a kind of morality, isn't it?"

"It's all I need," I told her. "But I haven't your guilt complex."

Her eyes flared a little. "Don't be so glib with words like that. This circulating library psychiatric phraseology is the mark of a boob, Brock."

"Honey, I had five years at Stanford. I was in the upper tenth of my class. Don't be so scornful. I'm not *all* physical."

She turned the omelet. "Five years wouldn't get you a doctor's degree. And without that, you shouldn't use words like 'guilt complex.'"

"Okay, I take it back. I haven't your caliber of conscience, then. How's that?"

"That's not true, either. You have too much conscience."

I went back to the front page, trying to ignore Jan as politely as possible. She wasn't really digging at me; she was digging at herself through me. The non-sport sections of the paper had nothing new in theory or fact about the murder.

Breakfast was unusually quiet, though she wasn't sulking any more. She was reading about the murder. I told her about the sport columnist's piece on Dom Ristucci and she read that.

When she'd finished, she asked, "He didn't get this information from you, did he?"

I shook my head.

"Because I remember that I told you, and I'd be sick if I thought that's where this—this monster had learned it."

"Think of young Ristucci," I said.

"I am. You're working on this, aren't you? You're working for Mr. Quirk?"

I nodded.

"I hope you find the killer. Not so much because of Johnny but because of this Dom. I'll hold my thumbs, Brock."

I did the dishes while she dressed. Then I kissed her on the forehead and went out into the sunny day. Next door, behind the wire-mesh fence, the Doberman stood stiff-legged, growling deeply in his throat and trembling, staring at me.

I went over to spit in his face.

A lot of the boys were there and I sat next to Dean McLaughlin, quite possibly the greatest center who ever played football. I asked him about team morale and he shrugged.

Tomorrow would tell the tale, he thought.

This was the chapel at Elysian Fields, and the body of Johnny Quirk was buried in flowers. I hadn't gone up to look at him; it's a thing I can't do.

Deacon Dan Towler gave us a short eulogy and a short prayer and then a minister said so much less in so many more words it was embarrassing to listen to him.

The pallbearers were one relative, one Ram, Deborah Curtis' brother and David Keene. The services at the graveside were even shorter.

There were reporters and photographers waiting on the driveway at the foot of the slope. A knot of Rams came down the hill near me and I looked over to see that Dom Ristucci was in the middle of the knot.

His teammates were giving him protection against the vultures of the press. That's who the ghouls were waiting for, young Ristucci.

To my right, one of the photographers jumped up on the hood of a car, to shoot over the heads of the beefy convoy. That made it my business, because it was my car.

I reached over and got one ankle and slid him off. His head bounced twice as he toppled and his camera went skidding along the asphalt of the drive.

He got up, full of fight, and the cameras all swung our way. And Dom and his buddies climbed into a big Lincoln while the attention was on me.

The photographer had drawn a right hand back, and I waited. He wasn't big enough to make the fist mean anything. He lowered the hand when he saw the size of me.

"My car," I explained. "What's your name?"

The Lincoln moved away and there was a shout. The photographer glared at me and then a reporter came over. "Oh, Callahan—" It was the man who'd waited at my car the night of the murder.

"I thought all vampires had pointed teeth," I said.

He looked at me condescendingly. "The brainwashed Dick Tracy. Can't you stay out of our way? All we're trying to do is our job."

"Douglas is hiring," I told him. "Don't cry on my shoulder."

He shook his head and his smile was sad. "Where'd we get off on the wrong foot, Brock? What's eating you this morning?"

"That piece in the *Times*."

"I don't work for the *Times*. And that piece you read isn't typical of the *Times*, and you know it. That boy's no more typical of the *Times* than Pegler is of the *Herald-Express*. Now let's grow up and talk like men."

I opened the door of my car. I climbed in and looked at him through the open window. "I'm working with the Beverly Hills

Police and we have nothing new to give you. If I get anything, I'll call you."

His gaze was cynical. "You can do better than that."

"So help me, that's the gospel. It's been a blank wall, so far. Unless there are things the police know that I don't."

His eyes were scornful, "So long, Callahan. I hope you need *us* some time."

I was doing very well, getting the police *and* the press against me. It seemed reasonable to guess I would never be rich. This morning it didn't bother me too much. I was alive and so was my girl and it was a beautiful day without a trace of smog.

I went back to the office to check my mail. There was a check from the father whose daughter's suitor I had investigated, the fastest pay I'd received in my short career. There was an ad from the Peoria School of Detection and Criminal Investigation, offering the cut-rate special at eight dollars and ninety-eight cents, including the embossed diploma on parchment, framed. It was probably just what I needed, but I mailed the whole thing to Sergeant Gnup of the Beverly Hills Police Department.

I heard footsteps in the hall and looked up in time to see Deborah Curtis open my door. She was in black; she'd been at the funeral. She paused in the doorway, her dark blue eyes wet.

I rose, and came over to fuss with my customer's chair. I couldn't seem to get a greeting out. She came over wordlessly and sat down. She was the girl who had called on me that first day, just after Johnny had told me about the note on the seat of his car. It was the one who "might" be engaged to him and who wanted to know where he had been the night before.

Silence, while I went back to my chair. Silence for seconds after that. And then her voice, muffled. "John was with a girl Sunday night, wasn't he?" It was as if our previous conversation had never been interrupted.

"I don't know," I said.

"Yes, you do. And he didn't go to any movie."

I waited until she looked at me fully. Then I asked, "Does it matter now?"

Her young, sensitive face was rigid. "It matters now. The memory of him is still alive."

"And you want to kill that?"

She didn't answer me. She looked like a girl in shock; her gloved hands were clenched in her lap.

I asked, "How do you know he didn't go to a movie?"

"My brother saw him at the Orleans Room. With some cheap tramp."

"And when did you brother tell you this?"

"Twenty minutes ago," she glared at me. "He told me some other things, too. John was no angel, was he?"

"I don't know," I said. "I've never met any angels. Why didn't your brother tell you this before today?"

"Men—" she said. "They stick together." She looked away from me. "In high school, when John got into that mess with the teacher, I could forgive him. He was young—" She took a deep breath. "But I'll bet there were a hundred repetitions of that I never heard about."

"Miss Curtis," I said quietly, "John Quirk is dead. And you have a life ahead of you. John was too rich to stay completely invulnerable, but he was as good as the rest of us and probably better than most of us. None of that matters now. What matters is that he's dead and you're alive and the world is full of worthwhile young men to love. Staining his memory won't do you a damn bit of good."

She glared at me, and stood up. "Men—" she said again. Her body shook in a convulsive tremor. "Damn you, all of you." She sent me one more murderous glare before stalking out.

Men . . . She was right, and women, too. They weren't much, but all we had except for kids. And the nasty thing about kids, they grew up into men and women. People are monstrous, but all we have, Deborah Curtis would learn in time. Nevertheless it nagged at me. Did this classy girl who belonged to Johnny's own Beverly Hills, Ivy League world know anything she wasn't telling?

I went down to the drug store for lunch. My fan wasn't behind the counter, for which I was thankful. I didn't want to talk about football today. The hippy bleached blonde who waited on me gave me a minimum of dialogue and a maximum of service.

From there I drove to the Orleans Room. The signs in front informed me that Cornball Thompson and His Cotton Pickers were the present engagement. They were, I knew, a twangy, raucous pick-up of local exhibitionists, currently the rave among Dixie adherents.

The big room was closed, but the smaller barroom was open. The bartender was attired in black trousers and a white jacket. Under the white jacket was a magenta oxford shirt. His tie was black knit.

"Did you work Sunday night?" I asked him.

"Are you a cop or something?"

I showed him my identification. "I'm working with the Beverly Hills Police Department."

"I worked Sunday night," he said. "Is it about Johnny Quirk?"

I nodded.

"I already told the cops all I know."

"And what was that?"

"You should know it, if you're working with them. Private man, are you?"

"Usually. Not on this. Do you have some beef against private investigators?"

"That's right. One of 'em fixed me real good in the alimony department."

"I never handle divorce work."

"So long," he said. "Come back with a cop if you want to talk to me." He turned away and busied himself with some bottles.

I said, "Johnny Quirk was a Ram. And so was I, once. His dad hired me to work with the Beverly Hills Department on this. I can come back with a cop, if you insist. Or I can hang you up on that ceiling fan if you get lippy."

He turned back to consider me. "A Ram? What's your name?"

"Brock Callahan."

"The Rock," he said, and there was some respect in his voice.

"Have you got any Einlicher?" I asked him.

He shook his head. "Miller, Schlitz, Acme in bottles. Lucky Lager on tap."

"I'll take a bottle of Miller High Life."

He put a bottle of it on the bar and the glass next to it. He said. "There's nothing to tell. The police wanted to know if anyone here had seen the guy who put the note in young Quirk's car. Nobody had."

"I see. Do you get much of that Beverly Hills trade?"

"I don't know where all the squares come from. That buddy of young Quirk's, that Pat Curtis, he's a Dixie hound, too. But they weren't together Sunday night."

"Who was young Curtis with?"

"One of his own kind, society girl. I don't know her name. Brown hair and brown eyes. A little stocky for my taste." Now we're getting somewhere, I thought, recalling Deborah Curtis' visit.

"I suppose there are gamblers who like Dixie, too?"

"I wouldn't know. I couldn't name you any who spend time here."

"Do you know Rick Martin?"

"Only by name. I never saw him."

"Who picks up your bets?"

He looked at me levelly. "We don't book here."

"Do you know Ned Allen?"

"In the sport pages. I never met him, either."

"Lenny Heffner?"

He shook his head. "Never heard of him."

"Do you know Miss Jacqueline Held very well?"

He frowned. "Jackie? That blonde with Quirk?"

I nodded.

He shook his head. "I never saw her without him. She was no Dixie lover. Liberace, that's her speed."

I sipped my beer; he washed glasses. Some seconds went by. I asked, "Did you like Johnny?"

He didn't look up. "He was all right. Never ran a tab, never screamed for service. He was a damned good customer."

"How did he hit you, personally?"

The man seemed puzzled. "People don't hit me much, *personally*. He looked clean and sensible. It's too bad he's dead but I'm not crying."

I finished the beer. "I'll bet you don't have many friends."

He looked at me blandly. "I don't need many. That'll be forty cents."

I gave him five of it in pennies and the rest in the dirtiest coins I could find. I went out and headed back toward Beverly Hills.

I went past the gateway to the Quirk estate and on the hill beyond it I saw what looked like a bronze Ferrari. I drove on to the entrance of this second estate. It was the home of Johnny's Deborah, and I turned in.

I continued around the house to the parking area in the rear and there was the Ferrari. A boy in white coveralls was bending over the hood. "Beverly Sports Car Club" was stenciled in scarlet script on the back of the coveralls.

He looked up as I drove into the parking area. He continued to watch me as I left the car and walked over to him.

His hair was black and short and curly, his eyes the same deep blue as his sister's. He stood motionless, a wrench in his hand.

"Pat Curtis?" I asked him, and he nodded.

I was close enough now to see the alligator upholstery in the Ferrari. I asked, "Johnny's car?"

He nodded. "He lent it to me Wednesday. I'm going to try to buy it from his dad. You're Brock Callahan, aren't you?"

"That's right. Your sister was in to see me around noon."

"Oh." He shook his head and expelled his breath. "Don't mind Sis. She's really gone over the edge."

"You didn't help her any, telling her about Sunday night."

He looked at me worriedly. "Maybe not. But I tried to. Damn it, Johnny's dead. I don't want her burning incense all her life."

"I see." I leaned a hip against the Ferrari. "I suppose you know a lot about Johnny that the police don't know."

His sister's eyes looked out at me from his face. "Nothing that would help. Johnny never told anybody everything. We were about as close as two guys could be, I guess, but I'm not sure I ever really got through to him."

Pat Curtis . . . The name came back dimly, and I asked, "Didn't you go to Princeton, too?"

His grin was wry. "That's right. In the T, I'm the flanker. In the single wing, I'm the blocking back. Beverly Hills High and Princeton, Johnny was always the star. But don't make anything out of it, Callahan; envy isn't one of my vices."

I looked past him to where some sandbags were piled behind a row of targets behind the garage. I nodded that way. "Rifle range?"

He seemed to have stopped breathing as he stared at me. "That's right. We used to have a club. We were always starting clubs, Johnny and I. This was the Beverly Rifle Club and we haven't used the range for years."

I didn't say anthing. I went over to the edge of the hill. Below, I could see the grove of eucalyptus where Johnny's mother was buried. Why hadn't Johnny been buried there? Because he had died there, probably. Or because his dad was jealous of his mother's love? Nice thoughts for such a sunny day.

Pat Curtis came over to stand next to me. "Easy shot," he said, "and that was one place where I had it all over Johnny. I could shoot rings around him."

I was turning to face him when the maid came screaming across the parking area. She was almost incoherent, but we finally made out that "Miss Deborah locked herself in the bathroom" and hadn't answered a summons to the phone.

We both sprinted for the house.

∽∽∽∽∽∽∽∽∽∽∽∽ *EIGHT* ∽∽∽∽∽∽∽∽∽∽∽∽

FROM THE WINDOWS of the den in the Curtis house I could still see the Ferrari, standing with lonely elegance in the afternoon sun. Pat was saying, ". . . don't think Johnny was too crazy about Sis. He and I hung around together and Sis got the idea Johnny was coming here mostly to see her, I think. God, she thought he was really special."

The doctor came in with his bag. "She'll be all right. We've got her cleaned out now. There wasn't enough iodine in that bottle to do it, even if we hadn't got here right away. You can talk to her now, if you like." He paused. "Be kind, Pat. Be very gentle."

Pat Curtis stood up. "I will, sir."

The doctor went out, and Pat looked at me. "From seven to eleven on Thursday night, I was at a meeting of the Beverly Sports Car Club. There are a dozen guys who will testify to that."

"All right, Pat. I'll want to check a couple of them. You can understand I have to, can't you?"

"I don't mind." He started for the door to the living room, and then stopped. "There's one thing I didn't tell the police. Johnny had bet a thousand dollars on the Rams last Sunday."

"Why didn't you tell the police that?"

"I didn't want to dirty his memory. He's not permitted to bet, is he?"

"With a friend? It happens all the time, Pat."

"This wasn't a friend. This was at some joint in Santa Monica."

"Lenny Heffner's place?"

"I don't know the name. Johnny told me they had the best

enchiladas in town; that's all I know about the spot. See you.''

He hurried out, and I went directly outside through the sliding glass doors of the den. The view spread in all directions from this knoll; I stood for a moment drinking it in before climbing back into the Ford.

I checked three of the boys of the Beverly Sports Car Club and they told me Pat had been at the meeting. I didn't think the boys would lie about it if he hadn't; Johnny had been a member, too.

Then I went over to North Crescent Drive.

Sergeant Gnup was there and looking unhappy, his soft mouth almost petulant. ''What's this bit about the photographer at the funeral?'' he wanted to know.

I gave it to him in detail.

He looked at me dolefully. ''You don't care much about making friends, do you, Callahan?''

I admitted that perhaps I didn't work at it as hard as I should.

''You're not a cop, you know, Callahan.''

I told him I had a license from the Attorney General's office which gave me the right to act almost like one. And what did he have that I should know?

''You tell me first,'' he said gruffly. ''Found out anything?''

I told him what little I'd learned.

''Did you check this Curtis boy's alibi?''

I nodded. ''Seems sound to me.''

Gnup frowned. ''Damned strange he didn't tell us about the bet, isn't it?''

''I don't think so. He didn't want to smear Johnny's memory. And now, what have *you* found out?''

He hesitated, and I didn't urge him. It was getting to a point where I didn't care if he co-operated or not.

Finally he said, ''And this Held dame walked into Lenny Heffner's joint, huh?''

I nodded.

''That could be our boy, that Heffner,'' he said thoughtfully. ''He's got no alibi for the time. And it figures that young Quirk would phone Martino if he had trouble with Heffner. Martino is a local man and an enemy of Heffner's.''

"Do you think Johnny knew they were enemies?"

"If he knew Heffner *or* Martino, he did. Neither one of them made any secret of it. Martino, now, has never gone heavy. But Heffner has. He put in four years on an armed asault rap."

"But was it Johnny who phoned Martin?"

"That we don't know for sure."

"No. And if Heffner had set up Martin as the patsy, he'd be damned sure to have an alibi ready, wouldn't he?"

"Maybe. Maybe he never figured we'd get around to him. He was out driving that day, he said, seeing some people. He won't tell us who the people were. He admits he drove along Sunset Boulevard, though he won't admit it was at that time."

"And he never admitted Johnny had booked a bet with him?"

Gnup shook his head. "That kind of makes Heffner the key, right?"

"Maybe. I favor Jackie Held, for some reason. She knew Martin, Johnny *and* Heffner."

"And Heffner knows everybody involved, too. And he's gunned before. I'll stick with him."

"You can have him," I said. "He's got a friend I don't think I could handle the second time. Jackie's smaller; I'll stick with her."

"All right," he said, "and keep us informed." He took a deep breath, and looked uncomfortable. "I guess I wouldn't have to tell you I'm not the fair-haired boy around here since young Quirk was killed. If you get something and it comes to me first, it isn't anything I'd be likely to forget. You could use a friend down here, couldn't you, Callahan?"

I nodded. "I could use a friend anywhere. I don't seem to have the personality that attracts people."

He looked at me bleakly. "I'm serious, Callahan."

The soft lips were firm and the flat nose had never seemed more pugnacious. He glared at me with the dangerous look of the frightened man.

"I can use a friend," I said quietly. "I'll keep in touch with you, Sergeant. And you can put in a word for me with your superiors."

He nodded and some of the hate went out of his eyes now that he had the upper hand again. He said, "Just don't go cute on me, Callahan. I'm not bright, but I'm steady and I've been here for a long time. I like the job."

I kept annoyance out of my voice. "Okay, Sergeant, I get the picture."

I started to leave, and he said, "That attempted suicide, do you think that could be phony? Kid stuff? Dramatics?"

"I think she meant to kill herself, Sergeant. She loved Johnny Quirk very much."

"Okay. Keep in touch."

"Yes, sir," I said, and went out quietly.

He was where I was—nowhere. Johnny underground and his killer still breathing the clear, free air enjoyed by our respected citizens.

And tomorrow we played the Philadelphia Eagles. Beating the Eagles has lately been something the Rams can't seem to manage. We can plaster teams that wallop the Eagles; the Eagles themselves don't fear us a bit. Well, it was only an exhibition game.

It was almost six o'clock and I was hungry. I drove out to Bess Eiler's, in Santa Monica.

I had a drink at the bar first, and a glance at a *Mirror* someone had left behind. The *Mirror's* so full of columnists, there isn't much room left for news. Johnny Quirk's death had been demoted to page three and there was nothing there I didn't know.

My ribs were still sore and there was a blue-black, tender bruise between the middle knuckles of my right hand. I contemplated having a second drink, but decided against it. Even a first drink of hard liquor is something I rarely permit myself.

And where would I go after dinner? To see Jan? To Malibu and the poker game? Or over to watch the triplex that housed Jackie Held?

A one-man office is too limited for a case that was growing as complicated as this one was. Jackie, perhaps, I could get to under certain conditions. But I didn't have the authority to go up against men like Lenny Heffner, nor the connections to learn the real story on him. And frankly, I didn't have the guts to go up against him without the connections or the authority.

I had a rather fragile tie to the Beverly Hills Police Department through my client's influence, but it wasn't a tie that would stand much stretching.

In the movies and on TV you will see private operatives who go charging into murder cases, sneering at officers of the law and contemptuously taking guns away from hoods. But the reality is something else. Policemen don't like private investigators within a mile of a murder case and no man alive is bigger than a forty-five. Or even a twenty-two, for that matter.

My two hundred and twenty pounds was no protection against a man (or woman) who had the mental equipment which would permit him (or her) to kill. Toughness is mental, not physical, and I'd never have been mentally tough enough to kill.

And unless I was, I was no match for killers.

The inner voice I'd heard before was now saying it again: *Get out of the racket, Callahan; you're not equipped for it.*

"Another of the same?" the bartender asked me.

"No, thanks," I said. "I think I'll eat now." Then I had a shrimp cocktail and a big filet and three glasses of milk. I was on a case and I like to eat good when the money's coming in.

Then, though the lure of Malibu was strong, I drove over to the triplex right off Pico.

There was no answer to my ring and I went back to the car to wait. It was only a little after seven; if she was out for the evening she wouldn't have left this early.

A chartreuse Lincoln convertible went past me down to the next corner, and there swung in a U-turn. It came up the other side of the street slowly and parked in front of the triplex.

It was some seconds before the girl behind the wheel got out and walked up toward Jackie Held's unit. I went across the street and waited next to the Lincoln.

She was a slim girl, dressed in green gabardine, and her hair was a dark and lustrous red. Her eyes I hadn't seen, but could remember as between gray and green. Moira Quirk.

A minute at the door and she came back. She seemed to pause when she noticed me next to the car, but then came the rest of the way at the same pace.

Her eyes didn't avoid mine. "Well, Mr. Callahan?"

"Good evening, Miss Quirk. Business with Miss Held?"

"*My* business, if any. Certainly not yours." Disdain dripped casually from her resonant voice.

"Then you won't mind if this visit of yours goes into my report to your father?"

Her gray-green eyes considered me thoughtfully. "Are you threatening me?"

"No, Miss Quirk. Seeking information is all."

Indecision flickered briefly on her thin and attractive face. Then, "That's what I came for."

"Perhaps I can help. What did you want to know?"

The indecision didn't show this time. "I don't think I care to tell you, Mr. Callahan. And do what you want to about your report. But remember that my father isn't very well right now."

"If you're in trouble—" I said, but she moved past me and climbed into the Lincoln from the curb side.

It went away and I went back to my car. I turned on the radio and waited. Maybe Moira Quirk was playing detective, but I didn't think so. It wasn't her kind of game. Maybe Jackie knew something about her and Moira was worried that it had been partially responsible for Johnny's death?

That was from left field. One fact I had—they were both trying to get a foothold in the theatrical world. Did they know each other? Or did one know something about the other that the police should know? If this last was true, it would be Jackie who knew something about Moira, putting us back in left field. But if the reverse were true, the police would have it by now.

So that was the way, pick up the theory out of nowhere and then try to substantiate it, like the new thinkers. I waited, running out of thoughts.

At eight-thirty, I decided I had waited long enough.

On the way to Malibu, I went past Beverly Glen, but I didn't turn in toward Jan's. I wanted to learn what the boys still active had thought about Johnny Quirk.

It was dark now, but not too cold, and the traffic was heavy along Highway 101. The lights of the Bay were clear, the breeze was soft and most of the convertibles had their tops down. Even so, a lot of the magic had gone out of this country. Too many people had moved in, bringing their dull minds with them.

In the hills above Malibu, in the impressive home of Don (Scooter) Calvin, the boys were assembled and talking and all the talk was Quirk.

They thought I knew things about him, which I did, and would divulge them, which I wouldn't.

"If you want revenge, deal," I said. "And if you know anything tell me. I'm working on the case."

"Dick Tracy," one said, and "Fearless Fosdick," another, and Scooter said, "Lay off the Rock, you slobs, and let's see the color of your money."

We played cards and talked. The talk went from Quirk to the Eagles to the rookies who were being dropped. And finally to Dom Ristucci.

Scooter said, "The kid hasn't found himself. And that piece about being related to Martino didn't help him any."

Somebody used a foul word.

"Dom will make out," Scooter said. "He's steady."

I said, "I heard rumors of dissension. Or read them, somewhere."

Six pairs of eyes looked at me pityingly. Nobody said a word.

"Well," I said, "I've been busy. How was I to know?"

The twelve eyes continued to consider me like a dozen consciences. The silent treatment, because I hadn't made the last Ye Olde Rams' dinner and I wouldn't tell them what I knew.

Just a gag, but I said with petulance, "All right, let's deal. Whose deal, what's the game? Let's *go*."

They were nicer, after a while, but I still wouldn't tell them a thing.

IN THE LOCKER room it was fairly quiet. Near the doorway Dean was putting on his pads with the weary air of a knight who had seen too many die.

He smiled at me. "Not *you?* Things can't be that rough."

"You're a very funny man," I said. "Where's Ristucci?"

"Over there, in the corner. He's already dressed. You'd think he was in mourning."

The bulky figure of Les Richter loomed near. "You're getting fat, Rock. You must be eating well."

"I'm six pounds under my playing weight." I made a face at him and went over to where Dominic Peter Ristucci was staring dismally out at nothing.

I tapped his shoulder and he looked up. His smile was brief. "I'm sorry. I didn't see you. You're Brock Callahan, aren't you?"

"That's right. What have you been doing, reading the papers?"

He frowned. "Why?"

"It's a bad town for that."

He shook his head. "I've been thinking about Enrico."

"What have you been thinking about him?"

The brief smile again. "I was thinking about a shotgun he gave me once. An imported gun, a beautiful gun." He took a breath. "He's not much of a man, is he?"

"There are worse. He's no murderer. He didn't kill Johnny; that much I'll guarantee you."

The brown eyes were suddenly bright with interest. "How do you know? Did they find the killer?"

"Not yet. Enrico is going to pay me ten thousand dollars

when I do, though. That is the gospel truth, Dom.''

Some resolution in the face. ''I guess there are worse than Enrico, right?''

''Many,'' I said.

His smile stayed longer this time. ''You should see that shotgun. From Holland. It must have cost a mint.''

''Rick's not cheap. And don't you like our new coach?''

''He's it. He's the greatest.''

''All right, then; you've got your own problems and Rick's got his. We never can seem to beat the Eagles, you know. It's mighty important that we beat the Eagles.''

''Sure,'' he said. ''But, Brock, pep talks haven't touched me since my second year at South Bend. I'm a pro, Brock; let's not get sentimental.''

''That's the way to be,'' I said. ''I just didn't want you to carry any theatrical adolescent ideas around.''

''All right, all right,'' he said. ''All right.''

Edgy now, and that's the way I left him, that's the way I wanted him. Pros don't get sentimental, except about winning.

In the stands, Jan said, ''You couldn't think to bring a hot dog along, I suppose? We *had* to come early, I suppose?''

''You didn't,'' I said. ''I'll go and get you the hot dog.''

The drum majorettes were cavorting; Johnny Boudreau's band was giving out with ''Dixie.'' It was early, but people were pouring in.

''Never mind the hot dog,'' Jan said. ''What did you say to Dom Ristucci?''

''I told him Rick wasn't the killer.''

''How could you tell him that? You don't know . . .''

''He does, now. My God, woman, these are the Eagles we're playing today. Do you want to lose to them again?''

And then they were coming out, the boys who'd made the grade, the boys who'd become men. From Notre Dame and Hardin Simmons, from Michigan and East Overshoe School of Mines, from Wisconsin and little Loyola. Some had been big in college and some of the colleges you've never heard of. And a few hadn't gone to college at all.

Some of them earned less here, as pros, than some of the

others had earned as amateurs in college. Money wasn't enough to make them play this game. There wasn't that much money. They played this game because they loved it and they wanted to extend their days of glory to the ultimate.

I knew about the braces some of them wore, and the elastic bandages. I knew the precarious rim of nausea some rode because a bad knee can kick out any time, and the contemplation is worse than the catastrophe.

Philadelphia had won the toss and they elected to receive. Les Richter would kick off. People were still pouring in as the ball was adjusted on the tee.

A lot of people missed the first score of the game. Because Jug Harter of the Eagles took the kickoff deep in his own end zone and decided to run it out.

From the ten-yard line to the thirty, he dodged and twisted like a dervish, trying to keep a blocker between him and every threat. From his own thirty, it was much simpler. He simply outran everbody to the goal.

The kick was good and, my neighbor said, "Same old story. The Eagles have our number."

"Maybe," I said.

Jug Harter came out as the platoons changed. He got a big hand from the stands.

"What are they cheering *him* for?" Jan asked.

"Because he looked so good."

"Lucky," Jan said.

Dom Ristucci wasn't coming out for the kickoff; Boyd and Quinlan were deep. Neither of them got a chance to touch the ball as it bounced past the end line.

Rams' ball, first and ten on their own twenty, and Dom Ristucci came trotting out.

"Now, we'll see," the man sitting next to me said.

The Eagles had evidently decided to cover the long passes. That had been the great Ram threat for years, the long pass. Dom tossed them short. To the flat and the little button-hooks right over the line, and he completed four out of five, and it was first and ten on the Ram forty-two when the Eagles called for a time out.

"He's not real flashy," my neighbor said grudgingly. "He seems solid, though."

"Professional," I said. "He knows what he's doing."

Time was in again, and that hoary old chestnut, the Statue of Liberty, was the next play. Quinlan took the ball from Dom's hand on the simulated pass, and swung wide toward end. It looked like he might make some yardage.

The defense swung that way. And the man covering Boyd looked back to see what was happening, and Boyd turned goalward and flew.

He caught Quinlan's pass on the twenty and romped to six points. And Jan screamed and my neighbor yowled and Boudreau's band screamed its challenge.

Les Richter's point-try tied it up.

This was the new day of the new Ram quarterback. As my neighbor had said, he wasn't flashy. But he was a stalwart, stocky, technician and behind him were the muscle-building vineyards of the San Joaquin Valley and four years of Notre Dame football tutelage. He was a cool and brainy boy, playing this game like the professional he was.

After that first run, the Eagles never led. They were no pushovers; it was never a runaway. But Dom built the Ram advantage up to ten points and played the points and the clock like a man in command. Which he was.

It was 38 to 28 when he came off and they gave him a standing ovation. The gun sounded two minutes later.

My neighbor said, "Well, we finally beat the Eagles. Watch out for us this year."

Jan and I went down the ramp in the sunlight and there was more chatter today. Last week they had seen a miracle; today they had seen a pro.

Ahead of us, walking laterally to our path, I saw Enrico Martino. Jackie Held was with him, hanging onto his arm. They went over toward a refreshment stand as we started across the blocked-off street.

And then I saw Curly, the boy I'd kayoed. With him was a slim and dapper man I'd never seen before, but I could guess he'd never turned an honest dollar.

I saw Curly nudge the little man and nod meaningly toward the refreshment stand. And I saw the trouble-seeking smile on Curly's face.

I said to Jan, "Wait right here, on the curb, by this tree."

And I went over to the stand. I got there before Curly had said a word, though Rick had seen him and they were eyeing each other.

I stood next to Martin and said, "Some game your cousin played. He's a real pro."

He'd glanced at me briefly. Now he nodded and kept his eyes on Curly. The little man was looking doubtful, but there was no doubt in Curly's smile.

Without looking at me, Martin asked, "Know him, Brock?"

Loud enough for all to hear, I said, "Not by name. I know he's got a glass jaw."

The little man looked more doubtful, Curly less.

"Pug Heffner, Lenny's brother. I wanted you to know his name in case something happens."

Heffner said smilingly, "What would happen, ginzo? Don't tremble, wop."

And then a voice said, "Who you calling wop, mister?"

I turned to see Tiny DePaolo standing there. Tiny's best days are a few seasons back, like mine, so he had put on perhaps ten pounds of fat. But a man who weighs three hundred and twelve pounds can use ten pounds of softening.

He saw me when I turned around, and he grinned. "The Rock. Hey, what goes? This midget giving your buddy trouble?"

Tiny stands six feet and ten inches high, which gave him a good eight inches on Pug Heffner. Though it didn't make Heffner a midget.

I said mildly, "I guess he doesn't like Italians, Tiny. I'll take the little one."

Rick Martin was smiling now. "I was sort of saving him for me, but if you insist. —"

The little man melted into the crowd. But I had to hand it to Pug Heffner. He stood where he was, facing close to seven hundred and fifty pounds of animosity.

Tiny said genially, "You meant *Italian*, mister, didn't you? The wrong words kind of slipped out, didn't they?"

"They weren't meant for you," Pug said.

"All right then, shorty. No harm done." Tiny waved at him with the back of his hand. "Run along, boy."

For perhaps five seconds Heffner stared at us, and then he turned and walked abruptly away.

I punched Tiny's arm. "Thanks. I don't think I could take that man again. How'd Ristucci look to you?"

Tiny closed his eyes in ecstasy. "How about that wop? How about that ginzo? What a sweetheart, huh? What a *sweet* paisan."

I introduced him to Martin and left them there. Jan was still next to the tree near the curb but she had evidently seen it all.

Because she said, "I thought you didn't like Rick Martin."

"I don't."

"You certainly went rushing to his defense quickly enough."

"A principle was involved," I said. "Rick was minding his own business and Pug Heffner was looking for trouble. You can understand that a principle was involved, can't you?"

"No. Because neither of them were concerned with *your* business."

"You're just jealous because Martin had the blonde with him. How about Milton's for dinner?"

She shook her head, saying nothing.

"You're not angry?"

She smiled, and shook her head again.

Sunday, September eleventh, this was. But following the pattern of Sunday, September fourth, and I had an eerie sense of being involved in a time warp.

"I wonder who'll die *this* Thursday," I said.

"Wh-a-a-a-t?" She stared at me.

"Nothing." I held the door of the car open for her. "You've got a date tonight, have you?"

"Hmmm-hmmm. Worried?"

I shook my head and said warmly, "I trust you, Jan."

The brown eyes flared for a moment, and then she got into the car and I went around to get in behind the wheel.

I turned on the radio and waited for the traffic to thin out.

After about a half-minute, she said, "There's a limit to how far you can go in the private investigation business, isn't there, Brock?"

"I suppose. But there's no limit in your dodge. And I'm not too proud to live off a woman."

"I'm being serious, Brock."

"All right. I'm sorry. Continue."

"How can I continue? There's nowhere to go. I wouldn't be happy married to a man content to wash other people's dirty linen for day wages."

"That's blunt enough," I said. "Would you be happy married to *any* man, Jan?"

"A man with ambition, yes."

I smiled. "You keep telling yourself. I've had an offer to coach at one of the valley high schools. Would you be content with that?"

"I don't think I could stand the high school faculty social life. And I don't think you could, either. Isn't there something you *want* to do, some profession or business you'd planned on as a kid?"

"None."

She sighed. "So where does that leave us?"

"Right here, waiting for the traffic to thin out."

Her voice was edged. "To use your words, that's blunt enough."

"Why should we con each other? I'm not ashamed of my work and I'm not particularly interested in getting rich. And neither are you, or you'd have married a rich man. Beverly Hills is full of them, and I'll bet you've had some chances."

Silence from her and her eyes were angry, staring out at the cars jammed for blocks.

"I love you, Jan," I said, "but nobody has ever *owned* me. With luck, nobody ever will. You can remake a drab house but not a man who'd be worth the effort."

"Save the cornball philosophy," she said bitterly. "I can do without that."

The radio was giving us the scores of the eastern N.F.L.

exhibition games now. The Giants had walloped the Browns 42 to 7. The Giants were going big this season, favored in the Eastern Division.

Traffic throbbed and squealed and roared and hummed. Jan was silent. The radio gave us Thompson and His Cotton Pickers on an obscure label, and I thought of the Orleans Room and Johnny Quirk.

"I should have been born rich," I said. "I haven't enough moral fiber to be a successful poor man."

Jan made no comment.

As a matter of fact, I didn't get another word out of her all the long and wearisome drive to Beverly Glen. There, as I dropped her off, I asked her, "Shall I call you? Or wait for your call?"

"It could be a long wait," she said, and went up the slope without looking around.

The Doberman next door was wagging his tail at her as I swung around and went back the way I'd come.

~~~~~~~~~~~~~~~ *TEN* ~~~~~~~~~~~~~~~

RICK MARTIN'S IMPERIAL was parked in front of Jackie Held's domain and I sat in my car for a few moments, wondering if this would be a bad time to go in.

I decided to take the chance that Enrico Martino was no matinée lover.

Jackie Held opened the door and her eyes were fearful. "I can keep a secret," I said quietly. "Busy?"

"Not exactly. Rick is here."

"I know," I said, and gave her the meaningful look.

Her face went blank. "Come in."

Rick Martin sat on the flowered davenport near the small, high-hearth fireplace, a drink in his hand. A squat bottle of Scotch was on the coffee table in front of him.

He grinned at me. "Some hunk of man, that DePaolo. I should hire him for a muscle."

"Poor Pug was outweighed, wasn't he? Is he Lenny's big threat?"

Martin nodded. "Drink?"

"Not unless you've got Einlicher," I said.

Jackie had gone over to sit near Rick. I saw her pale and the glance she sent me was pleading.

"Einlicher?" Martin frowned. "What's that?"

"A beer I like. Do Lenny and his brother get along?"

Martin held up two fingers intertwined. "Lenny's got the head and the ambition and Pug's got the muscle. What was that remark you made at the game about not being able to take Pug *again?*"

Jackie seemed to be holding her breath.

I told Martin about the incident in Heffner's bar, omitting only the presence of Jackie Held at the fracas.

Martin stared. *"You knocked Pug Heffner out?"*

I shrugged. "It was a lucky punch. I'm sure he could take me next time."

Martin nodded. "And you can be sure there'll be a next time. He has a considerable reputation to maintain."

"Can't win 'em all," I said, and looked at Jackie. "I've a feeling you're not telling me all you know about Johnny Quirk. All you know that would help us, I mean, of course."

She said nothing, staring at the coffee table.

Martin finished his drink. "Well, I've a card game I'd hate to miss. Perhaps you'll do better without me around, Brock." He stood up and smirked. "Jackie's kind of maidenly."

Resentment flared in her young-old face. "I thought we were going to Ciro's."

He looked down at her blandly. "Not tonight, honey. You've got your dates mixed up again."

"You're angry about something," she said. "Why?"

He smiled. "Believe me, I'm not angry. This card game is very important, honey."

She went to the door with him. There, over her shoulder, he said, "Luck, Brock. Keep in touch, won't you?"

I nodded.

For seconds after the door had closed behind him, she stood with her back to it, staring out at nothing. Dimly we heard the grind of his starter.

Then she looked at me. "Damn him. Damned dago thinks he's something, doesn't he?"

"He's achieved a certain eminence. He's equipped for it, mentally and physically. I mean, equipped to come up the way he did." I smiled at her. "You're not, Jackie."

"I don't know what you're talking about," she said. "I have some Einlicher he doesn't know about. Would you like a bottle?"

"I'd treasure it. Jackie, break down. Have a good cry and tell me all about it."

"You're crazy," she said, and went through the doorway to the kitchen.

Lambs who try to be wolves have always hit me where I'm softest. Jackie was one of these, I felt sure, wheeling and dealing, playing all the angles she could uncover. And losing.

When she came back in again, she had a frosty bottle of Einlicher and a glass. I was sitting at one end of the davenport; she put the bottle and glass down in front of me and sat at the far end, near the fireplace.

I thanked her and asked, "What happened after I left Heffner's last Friday?"

"Nothing. I finished my enchiladas and left."

"You didn't get any satisfaction from Lenny about that producer he knows?"

She didn't answer.

I said, "What were you going to trade Lenny for the influence?"

"Nothing. That damned dago—"

"Heffner?"

She lighted a cigarette. "No. I'm talking about Rick Martin, Enrico Martino, Mr. Sex Appeal. He thinks—"

I chuckled. "So it's not all dollars and cents, eh? You lust for him, do you?"

She turned her head to glare at me. "What's so damned funny about that?"

"I'm sorry. You're right; it's not funny." I sipped my beer.

"I'll show him," she said softly.

"Don't do anything foolish, Jackie. You're playing with some case-hardened characters."

"They don't scare me."

"That's your error. I weigh a hundred pounds more than you do, Jackie, and they scare the hell out of me. Why don't you have a drink and relax?"

She looked at me suspiciously. "Why should I? Why do you want to get me drunk?"

I shook my head and smiled. "I don't. I didn't think one drink would get you drunk. I've got a girl, Jackie; I'm not on the make."

"All men are on the make," she said, "all the time. But I'll have a drink." She put some ice in Rick's empty glass and poured Scotch over it. She leaned back and kicked off her shoes.

"Rick's handsome enough," I said. "I know he has a daughter; is he still married?"

She nodded. "To a tramp he hasn't seen in three years. She's in Europe. Rick doesn't want to divorce her. He says it's because of his daughter, but he lies. As long as he's married, nobody else can hook him."

"I see."

A silence, though I thought I could hear her simmer. I said, "If you got work at Twentieth Century-Fox, you could walk to work, couldn't you?"

Interest in her voice. "I certainly could. Do you know somebody there?"

"No. But I know the man who has the saddle-soap concession at Republic."

"You're *so* funny." She leaned forward to put more Scotch into her glass.

Silence, again, as she leaned back, sipping the drink. Then a chuckle. "That *was* kind of funny." She sighed. "I never laugh any more. This is a rotten town, isn't it?"

"Most big towns are. Where are you from?"

"Waukesha. That's in Wisconsin, in the prettiest part of Wisconsin. I couldn't take it, though. I couldn't go back to it."

"No Enrico Martinos there, eh?"

"To hell with Enrico Martino," she said, and finished her drink. She leaned forward to refill the glass.

"Easy, honey," I said. "Control, control, control—you can't let your emotions take over. This isn't Waukesha; you've got to play it the smart way."

"Don't worry." She started to sip, changed her mind and looked at me sharply. "Why should you worry about me?"

"Because you're a lamb among wolves. And as Mr. Saroyan stated, I'm always for the lambs and against the wolves."

"Saroyan? Who's he? Is he a producer?"

I sipped the beer and considererd her question. "No. He's a—uh—purple-foot from Fresno who should have stayed there. He's probably the only new talent in the twentieth century."

"An actor?"

"A writer."

"Ugh," she said, and sipped her Scotch. "Writers, they're the worst. They buy you a box of toffee and want to move in for the week end."

I said nothing.

"And the ideas they get!" She shook her head and grimaced. Her voice had sounded thick.

"If you haven't eaten," I said, "I wouldn't go after that Scotch too hard. It could knock you out."

"I had a hot dog," she told me. "Don't worry; I know when I've had enough." She curled her legs up under her. "Tell me how good I looked on Big Town again."

"I will if you'll tell me about Lenny Heffner. And anything else that's troubling you. You weren't with him Thursday afternoon and evening by any chance, were you?"

She looked at me owlishly. "Thursday I was out of town. I've got proof. Arrowhead. With a—a friend. Would you like another bottle of beer?"

"No, thanks. Jackie, can't you consider me as a friend, trying to help you? I'm very serious about this."

She said nothing, looking into her glass.

"You were home Thursday night. I was here."

"I got home at nine-thirty. The police know that."

"I see. And did you tell them about the friend you were with?"

"I did. It was Pug Heffner." Her chin lifted. "And we were seen together up there at Arrowhead. Is that alibi enough, Mr. Callahan?"

"That's alibi enough. For you *and* Pug. I thought it was Lenny you were interested in."

She looked at me coolly. "I'm interested in anybody who can help my career. And not saddle-soap salesman." She slurred the triple alliteration.

I finished my beer and stood up. "All right, Jackie. I won't crowd you. Be careful, though, won't you?" I smiled down at her.

She looked up at me doubtfully and then her face softened. "Don't go. Have another bottle of beer. Don't go yet. I don't want to be alone."

"Yes, you do. You decided that some time ago, Jackie."

She shook her head. "No. Please. Couldn't we go out and eat? Or I could fix something here?"

I studied her and said, "I'll have another bottle of beer. Shall I get it?"

She nodded. "It's in the refrigerator, in the crisper drawer, buried under the vegetables."

And maybe, I told myself, in the refrigerated Jacqueline Held there were other things hidden and another hooker or two of Scotch would bring them out. That's why I decided to stay.

It didn't work out that way. We talked around the subjects I was most concerned with. Alcohol dulled her mind and thickened her tongue, but it didn't break down her controlled wariness. Half an hour later she was asleep on the davenport.

I went back to her bedroom and brought out a quilt to cover her with. I made sure the night latch was on before closing the front door.

It was just growing dark and it was getting chilly. The huge Twentieth Century lot looked barren and deserted, which it was, today. At the municipal golf course across the street, there were still some cars parked and a foursome was putting on the eighteenth green.

I drove down to Ted's Grill in the Santa Monica Canyon. At Ted's you can get a steak cut and cooked to your own particular specifications, and I ordered a big one, medium rare.

Jackie, who'd planned on Ciro's, was at home alone and asleep. All I'd learned from her was that she had gone to Arrowhead with Pug Heffner and that she yearned for Enrico Martino. And that she had originally hailed from Waukesha, Wisconsin.

That wouldn't be considered first-class investigative accomplishment, but Jackie wouldn't be the easiest subject in the world for even an expert interrogator. I had got to her a few years too late. And without a casting couch.

It was dark now. From where I sat I could see the headlights on the Coast Highway. A moppet in the next booth stuck his head over the partition and considered me gravely. I winked at him.

I wondered what Jan was doing, *right now*. Getting ready for her date, or was her date already there? And if he was, what were *they* doing?

I thought about Mr. Quirk and Moira and Johnny and his girl. Deborah and her iodine, Jackie and her Scotch; sisters under the skin. The flavor was similar, too.

"Anything else, sir?" the waitress wanted to know.

"Another glass of milk, please," I said, and wondered how it would mix with Einlicher.

There was a light glowing in the dome of the portico at the Quirk house. Then a light showed through the glass of the front door and a few seconds later the door opened.

The butler said sadly, "Mr. Quirk is resting, Mr. Callahan. I'd rather not disturb him."

"Is Miss Quirk here?"

"Miss Moira went out about an hour ago, sir."

"Do you know where and with whom?"

"I don't, Mr. Callahan. She was going to meet some studio personage, I believe. But I'm not sure of it."

"She seems to have recovered from the shock of her brother's death."

He said nothing, his face a sad, black mask.

I said, "I'd appreciate if you'd let *both* of them know I was here. I think Miss Quirk would be interested to hear it, too."

He nodded gravely. "I'll see that they are both informed, Mr. Callahan."

I went back to the car and sat there for a while before starting the motor. Around and around and around and getting where? It was frustrating and enervating.

But something would break. Something *had* to break.

The headlights on the Ford swung out over the slope as I turned around, illuminating the eucalyptus grove where Johnny had died and where his mother was buried.

IT WAS A troubled sleep, filled with headstones and some other things I don't remember now. In the wakeful moments, I thought of the women in Johnny Quirk's life, his mother and Moira, his Deborah and Jackie Held, that overemotional high school teacher. And the others I'd only heard about, names without faces. A Ram he had been, all male.

I saw the lacquered face of the Waukesha wanton and heard her say, "Don't go. I don't want to be alone."

It was a muggy morning, with a low overcast. Even in Westwood there was a tinge of smog in the damp air. There was nothing new in the *Times* about the murder and I didn't feel ready for the sport-page account of yesterday's game.

I was out of cornflakes and out of milk and there was only one shriveled crust of bread; I ate breakfast at the drug store.

My fan said, "That Ristucci is going to make the grade, I think, don't you?"

I nodded.

"Those Notre Dame boys are pros in college, almost, right?"

"Almost. Scrambled eggs with bacon and a glass of milk."

"Check. What's the matter, Brock? You seem sour this morning."

"I had a bad night." I smiled at him. "I don't want to talk. Okay?"

"Check." He made the circle with his thumb and forefinger and went over to put in my order.

A man could ask questions until his voice gave out, but where would that lead? People innocent and guilty answer only out of self-preservation, telling you only as much of the truth as is convenient for them. And no one is completely innocent. Nor completely guilty.

97

Questions, questions, questions . . . I was sick of the sound of my own voice. Wasn't there any way to seek the truth without a barrage of questions?

In my cute little pine-paneled office it was quiet. From all the points of the compass people huffed and motors puffed, people bled, sweated, fought and made love. But in the egocentric center of the compass it was quiet, and I tried to think.

The vision of the Ferrari came to me, and I thought of Pat Curtis, brother of the beloved of the deceased. Mail slid through the slot of my office door and plopped on the floor.

Three ads and two bills. I made out a pair of checks for the bills and addressed and sealed a pair of envelopes to carry the checks to my benign creditors. And then, as my fingers warmed to the work, I typed the history of yesterday.

I got all my reports out, after that, and read the story of last week as seen through the eyes of a semiskilled investigator.

Nothing.

Pat Curtis stayed in my mind. I told my phone-answering service I'd be gone for less than an hour and walked over to David Keene's bookstore.

David was reading this morning, for which he wore horn-rimmed glasses. He looked scholarly and adjusted in his small office. The book was a title I've forgotten by a man I didn't know.

"There's a man troubling me," I said. "A young fellow named Pat Curtis."

Keene smiled. "Troubling you? Pat? He's the original All-American boy; there's nothing wrong with Pat."

"He isn't the All-American boy," I corrected him. "Johnny was that. Pat is perhaps the envious buddy of the former All-American boy."

David Keene frowned. "Oh, no. No, no, no, that's way out of character. Pat is a completely extroverted, very happy lad without a smidgin of envy. You're reaching, Mr. Callahan."

"Maybe," I admitted. "But Johnny was practically engaged to his sister and chasing around with other women. And young Pat always lived in Johnny's shadow; he admitted that to me."

"He wouldn't have admitted it if he were guilty."

"Maybe not. Or maybe he's cleverer than we think. And he's a fine rifle shot, he admitted, and the place where Johnny died is an easy rifle shot from the Curtis estate. Easy for an expert, that is."

Keene's frown was deeper. "Did you talk to Pat about all this?"

"I did. And he's got a dozen lads from the Beverly Sports Car Club to alibi him. Do you know any of that gang?"

"I might. I suppose I do. Could you name me a few of them?"

I gave him the names of the boys I'd talked to.

"Fine families," David said. "And good, solid boys. They might lie for a friend, but not to cover a murder, I'm sure."

"Which leaves me where?" I said. "*Somebody* killed Johnny."

Keene nodded thoughtfully. "And I'd hate to be the man who had to investigate it. Johnny had so many facets, so many worlds." He shook his head. "And he had a core of secretiveness in him that very few people ever penetrated, I'd bet."

"Maybe nobody ever penetrated it."

Keene nodded again. "That could be. But with some of the trash Johnny seems to have mixed with lately, I'd consider Pat Curtis a bad choice as a suspect."

"Name me a good choice. Rick Martin?"

He shook his head. "The man couldn't be that much of a fool. Some enemy of Martin's, I'd guess."

"How about Moira Quirk?" I asked. "She associates with some of the trash element, possibly."

He shrugged. "Moira's always been—an individual. She never cared much for the Junior League ratrace or the other artificialities. She's a very intelligent girl, Mr. Callahan."

"I didn't know intelligent girls yearned to be movie stars."

He smiled. "Why not? I've been called intelligent, but I'd trade with Tyrone Power right now. Wouldn't you?"

I shook my head. "Though I'd probably trade with Les Richter right now."

He sighed. "All right, Les Richter. We all want different things, I guess. And I'd rather be Faulkner than Power, too, I guess."

"And how about Johnny?" I asked him. "What do you think he wanted to be?"

"Back in the womb. Or maybe just exactly what he was, quarterback for the Los Angeles Rams."

Silence.

Then Keene said, "One thing I'd keep in mind, Johnny probably confided a lot more in women that he did in men. Most of the really manly boys do." He looked down at his desk top. "I've been thinking about that phrase 'the day of the ram.' That would apply to our time, wouldn't it?"

"How do you mean?"

"I mean, it's a period in our history when athletic prowess gets undue admiration. A bookseller in the east who recently went out of business called this 'the age of the boob.' The athlete has taken over the public interest and the racketeer is moving in to get his cut."

"Wherever there's money, there are going to be hoodlums," I said. "Even in the publishing business. How about the trashy magazines and books that are flooding the market?"

Keene smiled. "Touché. All right, a truce. Your voice was shaking."

I smiled back at him. "I think yours was, too. But now that I'm here, how about some 'feelthy peectures'?" I stood up. "I'll probably be back. You help me to think."

"Thank you, sir. Nine to six, any day but Sunday. And if you ever need a book or magazine subscription . . ."

I waved, and left the vicarious world of David Keene for the smog-tinged haze of the sidewalk. I went back to the office.

There wasn't anything to do there and I wasn't being paid by Mr. Quirk to sit there, so why did I? I had a place to go.

But I didn't want to go there. I'd been ordered out of the place last Friday and wouldn't be welcomed today. Especially not since the incident of the refreshment stand. I had no weapon that could force the truth from the Heffners. Even the police had no weapons like that.

I strapped on my own weapon, a thirty-eight Colt Police Positive, and went down to my waiting steed.

• • •

Manny Cardez was again behind the bar. But his denim slacks were charcoal today, and the T-shirt was dark blue. He still wore the blue suède fruit boots with the crepe soles.

He looked at me doubtfully. "You've got a nerve coming here. I'd get in trouble if I served you."

"Don't serve me then. Run in and tell the Heffner brothers I'm here on a social call." Unlike me, my voice was poised and cool.

Manny studied me. "Why don't you leave them alone? They're not killers, either one of them."

"I'm glad to hear that," I assured him. "Are you afraid to take a message to them?"

"I was thinking of you. You're number one on Pug's list of unfinished business."

"Don't worry about me; I'm armed. I'm waiting, Manny."

He paused for a moment, studying me quietly. Then he went the length of the bar and over to the door with the frosted-glass panel. He opened it wider, this time, and I could see it led into a hallway.

Out in front a bakery truck was stopping, and I watched the driver unload a basket of bread and deliver to the door that must have served the kitchen.

The driver had come out and driven away before Manny returned. Manny gestured toward the open door. "At the end of the hall, the door to the right, the steel one. They're waiting in there."

The steel door had a peephole at eye level and I was conscious of the eye there before it swung open. It opened into a room with one high, barred window and some long tables on which there were a number of telephones. Three men I'd never seen before were busy on three of the phones. There was a pot-bellied stove in a corner of the room.

Lenny Heffner had opened the door and he gestured for me to follow him through another.

I followed him into a small office equipped with a steel desk, two steel filing cabinets and three chairs. One chair was behind the desk, one in front of it and one at a corner of the desk. The one at the corner was occupied by Pug Heffner.

Pug looked at me without expression. Lenny went around the desk to sit in that chair and indicated that I should take the third.

When we were all seated he asked, "Now, what are you looking for?"

"Just the warmth of a friendly voice."

Pug grunted. Lenny said, "C'mon, Callahan. Speak your piece. It's a busy morning."

"All right then," I said, "I'm interested in the death of Johnny Quirk."

"That shouldn't bring you here."

"Why not? It could very well be a gambling kill and you know most of the gamblers around town."

Pug said, "And you think we'd squeak, if we did?"

"It wouldn't be a bad idea. There's a lot of money represented in Quirk and his friends. And a lot of influence. If this killing goes unsolved, there'll be a lot of pressure on the department to clean up gambling."

Lenny's smile was thin. "*Which* department? He was killed in Beverly Hills. And right now you're sitting in Santa Monica."

"That's true enough. And Johnny had a thousand-dollar bet with you on the Ram-Bear game. The local police should be interested in learning that."

Silence. I thought I could hear Pug breathe. After a while, Lenny said, "Who told you that?"

"An informant I'd rather not reveal."

Pug said, "C'mon, Callahan. We've only got so much patience, you know."

"Nuts," I said.

Pug came halfway out of his chair, and Lenny barked, "Watch it, Pug. *Sit down.*"

Lenny's bald head glistened in the light from overhead and there was a queer glint in his blue eyes. Pug subsided in his chair, grunting something.

Lenny said quietly, "Who told you about the bet, Callahan?"

"Johnny did," I lied. "The morning after the game, when he came to see me with that note."

"Johnny Quirk came to see you?"

"That's right."

"Were you working for Martino then?"

"Not then and not now."

"You're a liar," Pug said. "Lenny, what the hell are you humoring this slob for? Leave me toss him out."

"I came prepared for a return match," I said. "I brought a thirty-eight along. And I've a license for it."

Lenny's smile was cool. "He brought a gun. Into our little bar and restaurant he comes, brandishing a gun. It's a good thing we overpowered him, isn't it?"

"Into your little bookie joint—" I started to say, and something clipped me right behind the ear.

I was still half-conscious and I started to get out of the chair. Pug was up now, and he brought an overhand right up with him, aimed at my jaw.

I twisted clear of that, but the force of his swing brought his body into me, and I went over backward with Pug on top of me.

I didn't have the moxie; that first blow had drained my fine, full strength. I tried to push him off, but my muscles were rubber. I saw Lenny overhead, too, now, and saw him swing his foot and felt the weight of it in my ribs.

I tried to pull my legs up to protect my groin and possibly use my feet as weapons. Pug drew back, away from me, taking his right fist along.

It was a bull's-eye. They were all over me and I guess I was out for a few minutes.

TWELVE

THE CHIEF OF the Santa Monica police was certainly a dandy. A little man with an unctuous voice, looking at me across his big, expensive desk, and sadly shaking his head.

"What else could we think, Mr. Callahan? a respected businessman in our community claims you came in brandishing a weapon. Whose story would you believe, if you were in my position?"

One tooth was loose. My lower lip was puffed and at least one of my ribs seemed cracked. There was an egg behind my ear.

"Since when is a bookie joint a respected business?" I asked him.

He frowned at me, horrified. "Evidently you don't know our little town."

"I read about it," I said, "but the writer called it Bay City."

"There's no gambling, not here, not while I've been chief."

"Yes, Virginia, there is a Santa Claus," I said humbly.

His soft, politician's face stiffened. "Are you being insolent, Mr. Callahan?"

"I can't think of any other way to get through to you, Shorty. Would you like to take a walk with me over to this respected business establishment? I'd like to show you a police-proof steel door and a roomful of telephones. Even you might get the significance of that."

I thought for a few seconds he was going to explode. His face turned scarlet and his soft hands clenched on top of his desk and his glare was at full wattage. He took a deep breath and fought his true, base nature.

"We can book you," he said. "I phoned about you and you

come well recommended. But we can book you, and don't forget it.''

"You didn't phone all my friends," I said. "The man I'm working for could buy this silly little town of yours."

His voice was controlled. "You've suffered a severe beating, and you're not yourself, I'm sure, Mr. Callahan. But I won't take *one more insolent word from you.* That's fair warning now."

"Fair enough," I said, and stood up. "My client is a very good friend of the Governor's. I'm sure he'll hear about it."

"And my *best* friend, Mr. Callahan, is the Governor's son-in-law. So there really isn't any reason for all this animosity, is there?"

"It's certainly not getting us anywhere," I agreed. "I hope you won't mind if I use your beach some time. I wouldn't want to be barred from such a garden spot."

He smiled. "Any employee of our Governor's friend is always welcome here. Good day, Mr. Callahan."

I nodded to him, and pain slashed from behind my eyes to the back of my neck. I fought nausea, walking very carefully out of his office and down the hall. I was looking for a door all the time.

I found it and made it, made the cubicle before letting go. I rinsed out my sour mouth and bathed my face with paper towels soaked in warm water.

In the spotted mirror I studied my puffed lip. I tried to twist around enough to see the lump behind my ear, but couldn't manage it. I thought of Manny Cardez, standing there in his immaculate cottons, lying to the patrol officers, his open, honest face giving substance to his oral fantasies.

I ached and throbbed and pulsated with pain but I couldn't feel too sorry for myself. I was old enough to know you can't beat city hall.

I hadn't felt this bad since the Lions worked me over in '53. I looked at myself in the mirror and saw the resentment in my eyes.

Easy, Callahan, play it cool, now. You're supposed to be a pro.

I rearranged my face to the pattern of an adjusted citizen and went out to the Ford. One of the patrol officers had driven it over from where it had been parked and the keys were above the visor.

I still had my gun and the license to use it, but the license didn't cover murder. I resisted the urge to drive back to Heffner's. It wasn't too persistent an urge to resist. I wondered if Pug and I would ever have a rubber match. I'd been lucky the first time and he'd won with a sneak punch the second time. I wasn't looking forward to a title engagement.

Rick Martin's home was in the recent California pattern, antiqued barn siding and heavy thatch roof, a sprawling, one-level place of about four thousand square feet.

The Filipino who answered the door eventually ushered me into a rear living room that overlooked a blue-slate patio around a fifty-foot pool. Martin was sitting near the open glass doors that led to the patio.

He looked at my puffed lip. "Well." He stood up. "What happened?"

I told him all of it, including the farce in the Chief's office.

He shook his head. "Sit down, Brock. Drink?"

"No, thanks." I sat down on a plastic upholstered love seat.

He met my gaze fully. "You look dangerous at the moment. You've a lot of belligerency in you, haven't you?"

"Right now, you mean?"

"Always."

I shrugged. "I guess. I don't relish being manhandled by hoodlums. And I don't see any way to get any further with them than I have. I thought you might be able to think of a way."

He smiled. "I'm glad you're on my side right now."

"I'm not. I'm not working for you, Rick. I'll take what help or information you can give me, but we'll never be brothers."

He was silent, staring out at the pool.

I said, "You must have some employees working for you, haven't you?"

He didn't look at me. "Very few. I'm more or less retired."

"Do any of the few that are left carry guns?"

He shook his head. "I was never heavy." He turned to face

me. "Do you have the idea I'm holding something out on you?"

"I consider it a strong possibility. That's why I came here."

"I know nothing," he said, "and that's why I wanted to hire you. Not as a gun or a muscle, but as an investigator, searching for all the truth you could find."

He sounded candid and earnest. But so do TV pitch men. But I took the chance, after a moment's consideration.

I said, "Did you know Jackie Held is a good friend of the Heffners? She was there the day I had my first run-in with Pug."

He stared at me. Finally he whispered, "The little bitch . . ."

"Remember, you're never heavy," I cautioned him. "And here's something else I learned—Johnny Quirk had a thousand-dollar bet riding on the Rams in that Bear game. The Heffners booked it."

He shrugged. "They wouldn't kill a man for a grand. But that other, about Jackie, that really burns me."

"Why? You're not emotionally involved with the girl, and as long as you're retired, she couldn't have any secrets to carry to the Heffners."

"Look, I was paying the girl's rent, wasn't I? And she knew how I hated the Heffners."

"That's adolescent," I told him, "and you know it. When did you start to hate the Heffners?"

He looked out at the pool again, and his voice was quiet. "I didn't start it. I took a girl away from Lenny, a girl he really carried the torch for. I—married her."

"You're still married to her?"

He nodded. "Though I haven't lived with her for five years. She's been in Spain for the last three."

"She's the mother of your daughter?"

He looked at me again. "That's right. And the only reason I haven't divorced her. She's given me enough cause for divorce."

"Simple reciprocity, then," I said. "I mean, Pug Heffner moving in on Jackie. She was up at Arrowhead with him Thursday."

His face was again composed. "I'll let him take over her rent."

"And go no further than that," I told him. "Because if you should harm her, I'd feel guilty about telling you what I did."

He frowned. "Why should you worry about her?"

"Because she's a woman. That might not mean much to a man like you, who has dealt in women as a commodity. But I'm still a little old-fashioned."

His voice was tight. "Easy, Callahan. I've got a daughter, remember."

"I've got a million daughters," I said, and stood up. "You wouldn't want me to learn tact at my advanced age, would you?"

"No," he said wearily, "I suppose not. You'll never be rich, Callahan."

"So I've been told before." I fingered the bump behind my ear. "You're sure there's nothing you want to tell me? I can keep certain secrets. Johnny Quirk's death has become personal enough for me to surrender a few ethical standards."

"There's nothing," he said quietly. "So help me, I'm in as much of a fog as you are."

"And you won't be rough on Jackie?"

"Not physically. I promise."

I'd left my breakfast in Santa Monica and it was past lunch time. The nausea was gone and I was hungry. I drove over to Cini's, thinking of the first time I'd run into Rick Martin, and how I'd slapped his face.

And how he'd promised I'd have reason to regret it.

His attitude had changed since then. That could be because of the change in mine. Or his learning of my few influential connections. Or perhaps, under his new Beverly Hills veneer, Enrico Martino was playing me for a patsy. I never felt comfortable around him.

Spaghetti and garlic bread with a bottle of beer, and back to the wars.

At the West Side Station of the Los Angeles Police Department, Captain Apoyan listened to my sad story of the brutal Heffners.

Then he put the tips of his fingers together and studied them. "What do you want me to do, Brock? This isn't Santa Monica."

"I know that. But they're always screaming about co-operation, aren't they? And I live in West Los Angeles, don't I? And Sergeant Pascal will tell you about Jackie Held. She lives in West Los Angeles, too, and her being a friend of the Heffners could tie in with the Quirk murder. That's what I was investigating over at the Heffners'."

"The Quirk murder isn't our baby, Brock. That's a Beverly Hills problem."

"All right, Pontius Pilate." I started for the door.

"Easy, boy," Apoyan said soothingly. "Now, don't go rushing off."

I turned around to face him, waiting.

"I'll send Pascal over to talk to the Heffners. But he'll have to take a local man along with him. They're very touchy in that snug little village."

"All right. Thank you, Captain."

His smile was somber. "Such a big man to have such a little brain. Why didn't you come to us *before* you went to the Heffners?"

"I wasn't sure you'd co-operate. And I went there in good faith, not hunting trouble."

"But armed?"

I didn't answer.

He said, "Stick to hotel skips and credit investigations, Brock. Leave the tough stuff to the experts."

I said nothing.

He looked at me levelly. "In our part of town, anyway. Am I coming through?"

"Yes, sir," I said.

He waved me out. I'd helped him plenty the last time we'd met, but there is something about the private-enterprise detective that brings out antagonisms in the municipal man. Maybe they resent our freedom from the time clock, or maybe it's the many charlatans in my trade. Whatever the reason, their attitude has the effect of putting us on a narrow ridge between the rascal and the law. It was easier for my kind to fall among the rascals; our work was more appreciated and the pay was better.

This country would be as badly off without private investigating agencies as it would be without private schools. There was too much work to be done for the taxpayer to carry the entire burden.

At least, these are the things I try to tell myself. The reality could be that I never outgrew my cops-and-robbers stage.

Somewhere, the killer of Johnny Quirk was laughing at all of us. Sergeant Gnup might be closer to a solution than I was, but I doubted it. And I had no place to go.

Back at the office, I phoned the Quirk home and asked for Moira, but she was out and the maid didn't know when she would be back. She took the message.

The deceased had been too active; he'd lived in too many worlds. From the cradle to the brothel, women had been very important to him, but he was still a man's man in the better sense of that phrase.

His secrets had been buried with him; the picture I had of him had come from too many divergent sources to be unified or true.

Motive, means and opportunity, the deadly triplicate necessary to murder. Rick Martin had the opportunity; he was on the scene. And quite possibly a motive if he was lying about his unconcern for Jackie Held. But means? Where was the gun? No, Martin had been the patsy, either intentionally or not.

Who had all three—motive, means and opportunity?

Pat Curtis had his alibi and Pug Heffner his. And Pug's included Jackie Held's.

Pug Heffner was a shield I couldn't pierce; I'd have better luck with Jackie if I gave her concentrated attention. I phoned her, and there was no answer.

I was sick of driving around the suspicion circuit, but I drove over to park in front of the triplex off Pico, anyway. Somebody else was already parked in front.

It was the chartreuse Lincoln convertible and Moira Quirk was sitting behind the wheel.

I parked behind and went over to her car to open the door on the curb side. Her radio was on and she was smoking. She looked at me without interest.

"Maybe we could wait together," I suggested.

"I don't mind." Her trained voice held an intriguing timbre.

I sat in the seat next to her and closed the door. "Want to tell me about it?"

She leaned forward to snap off the radio. "I came to ask her about John."

"You mean you think she knows things about him that you don't?"

She didn't look at me. "That's correct. She meant a lot to John."

"Probably no more than a hundred of her kind he's met before."

She shook her head. "John never told me about the others. He talked about Jackie frequently."

"Why? She's certainly nothing special."

"Johnny thought so. Do you know where she's from?"

"Waukesha, Wisconsin."

"That's right. And my mother was from Pewaukee, practically next door to Waukesha." Moira's voice was bitter. "Even in that, John saw some kind of symbolism."

"For God's sake," I said.

Nothing from Moira Quirk.

"This is ridiculous," I said. "And if Jackie does know something about—about what happened, why should she tell you things she wouldn't tell the police?"

Moira's thin face was cynical. "Because I can offer money, and introductions to important studio people."

She threw her cigarette out onto the street and pressed the selector bar on the car radio. A news report, courtesy of Anti-Paino, came on. The warm voice of the announcer explained how Anti-Paino was better than aspirin in seven highly important ways. Doctors recommended it.

The newsletter gave us the foreign, domestic and local news without any word devoted to the Quirk murder. Moira snapped it off.

I asked, "How long have you been waiting?"

"About twenty minutes."

"Are you sure the bell rang?"

She nodded.

"Maybe she's just not answering it. I had a feeling, when I saw her last night, that she was frightened of something."

"You could try."

I went along the walk that skirted the first two units and up onto the porch. I could hear the door chimes when I pressed the button.

I waited, and was about to turn away, when the dog began to howl. The sound seemed to come from the back yard of the house next door, but it sent a shiver of premonition along my spine.

I went to the living-room window, but the drapes were drawn too tightly. Then, I remembered the high window at the end of the dining room and I walked around to that.

It was too high for me, but I brought a galvanized ash can over from next to the incinerator and stood on that.

I could see Jackie Held now. Stretched out on the living-room floor.

I went back to the Lincoln and told Moira, "Get out of here. Get out of here right now. And don't tell anybody you were here. I won't either."

She stared at me, an unspoken question in the stare.

"She could be dead," I said. "But dead or not, it's no place for you. Think of your dad, and what a holiday the papers would have if it was known you were here. Beat it!"

I slammed the door of her car and waited until she was around the corner before going next door to phone the police.

≈≈≈≈≈≈≈≈≈≈ *THIRTEEN* ≈≈≈≈≈≈≈≈≈≈

CAPTAIN APOYAN LOOKED at the shade gently flapping in his office and back to some papers he was studying. I sat on a straight-backed chair pretending I didn't know he was ignoring me.

Sergeant Pascal came in and put some reports on his desk, gave me one loaded look, and went out again. Apoyan seemed very interested in the new reports.

I said, "It's your baby now, Captain. Remember, this afternoon you told me it wasn't your baby?"

He looked up thoughtfully. "Yes, I remember. She was poisoned late last night, it seems. Conine in that beer, that—" He frowned.

"Einlicher?" I asked.

"That's right. How did you know?"

"It's my favorite beer. No bars sell it, except for Lenny Heffner's bar in Santa Monica."

He nodded. "Your favorite, eh? When was the last time you had some of it?"

Very casual question, and loaded right to the last syllable. They probably had my prints on the bottle I'd had last night at Jackie Held's.

I pretended to give it some thought. "Let's see, I had a bottle at Heffner's a few days ago, and then—oh, I remember, I had a bottle at Jackie's place late yesterday afternoon."

His brown Armenian eyes seemed to devour me. "Try not to be too casual, Brock."

"You too, Captain," I said. "You know my reputation and I resent trick questions."

His face showed no emotion. "Was it a party at Miss Held's late yesterday afternoon?"

113

"Just Miss Held and I."

"Could it have lasted as late as, say, midnight, or perhaps beyond that?"

"No. I was at Ted's Grill by nine o'clock, and in bed by ten-thirty."

"Alone?"

"I always sleep alone, Captain."

"That's unfortunate," he said. "Alibis are important in murder cases." He stood up. "And you working for Rick Martin, and all."

"I'm not working for Rick Martin, Captain."

"We'll see about that. We've sent for him. In the meantime, Officer Caroline will show you your cell."

Officer Caroline was a fat man with a bad case of B.O. and no warmth in his heart for Brock Callahan. He now stood in the open doorway.

Captain Apoyan had sat down again, giving all his attention to the papers on his desk.

I said, "I want to phone my attorney."

Caroline asked, "Okay, Captain?"

Apoyan nodded without looking up.

I went out to the corridor with Caroline and down to a pay phone. From there I phoned Tommy Self. Tommy had learned his football with me at Stanford. But his law he had learned at Harvard.

I had just missed him, his secretary told me. He was on his way home. I told her my story and asked her to relay it to him at home as soon as he got there. She promised she would.

I tried to keep upwind from Caroline all the way to the cell block.

There, as he clanged the door behind me, he asked, "Anything witty to take back to the boys in the squad room, Callahan?"

I smiled at him through the bars. "I'm glad I use Dial soap. I just wish that everybody did."

It didn't come home to him. He shook his head and went down the corridor, out of sight.

I still had the lump on my head, the puffed lip, the loose tooth, the sore ribs and the blue-black mark between my knuckles. To this was now added an ache in the bad knee and a growing headache.

Footsteps along the corridor and the long, sour face of Sergeant Pascal came into view. "This girl got any parents, relatives, Callahan?"

"Her father's dead. I don't know about her mother or other relatives."

"Where is she from originally?"

"Waukesha. That's in Wisconsin, the prettiest part of Wisconsin."

He looked at me suspiciously. "It's hardly a time to be flippant."

"I was just remembering her words, Sergeant."

"You're chin-deep in hot water. You know that, don't you?"

I didn't answer.

"The Captain warned you only this afternoon about steering clear of murder cases."

"I promise not to report any more dead bodies I find in your district, Sergeant."

"You're too lippy, Callahan."

I said nothing.

His voice went on. "I was never in your fan club, but tying up with a hoodlum like Martin was further than I figured you'd go."

I yawned.

"What's the matter, did you lose your voice?"

For answer, I went over and flushed the growler.

He glared at me for seconds. Then he said, "We know how to handle insolence, Callahan." He went back up the corridor.

They certainly didn't know how to handle taxpayers. Well, Tommy would come down and smooth things over. Tommy belonged to the Young Republicans and the Old Democrats, Lions, Elks, Rotary, Odd Fellows, two beach clubs and one country club. He had a soothing voice and a quick mind and had been the greatest in a long line of great Stanford quarterbacks.

Tommy would straighten everything out. I kept telling myself.

But if I told Tommy Self about Moira Quirk, he would insist

that I tell it to the police. He works that way, with the police completely, because of his great regard for the law. And I didn't see any point in telling the police about Moira Quirk.

That sad man, her father, was carrying enough of a cross right now. And I was working for him. And only an idiot or a Caroline would consider her a suspect, sitting so innocently in front of the deceased's home.

Of course, there were always neighbors, and chartreuse Lincoln convertibles are not the most common cars in town. . . .

Some drunk a few cells down began to sing. The singing stopped and he began to moan. The moaning stopped and the silence was heavy.

I began to grow annoyed. A little disciplinary gesture like throwing me into the can for five minutes I could understand. This was getting too boring, forcing me to sit alone with my thoughts. My watch told me it had been an hour and a half ago that the aura of Caroline had gone away.

Then, just as I had decided to bellow, I heard footsteps again and hoped they were for me.

They were the nimble feet of Tommy Self and he looked abashed. "Sorry, Brock. I stopped off at the Club for a drink on the way home."

"Which of your many clubs did you favor this evening?"

He ignored that. "I talked to Mr. Quirk. He'll write a blank check and we can fill it in for any amount of bond they want."

"To hell with that. They haven't any reason to hold me."

"Enough. What *didn't* you tell them, Brock?"

"They know everything I know, and probably more. I tried to get Apoyan interested in the Quirk case this afternoon without success. This is the thanks I get."

Tommy sighed. "Where's the turnkey? Martin's here with his lawyer and there'll probably be a conference." He looked up the corridor. "I thought the turnkey would be here."

Then there were footsteps again and an officer came along with a key. He swung the door open and nodded for me to precede him.

As soon as I stepped into Apoyan's office I felt better. The atmosphere of the room was lighter; neither Pascal nor Apoyan looked as hostile as they had before. Rick Martin was sitting in there, and next to him was the town's most famous attorney.

Captain Apoyan said, "I've just had a phone call from Lieutenant Remington, Brock. Why didn't you tell me you were working for the Beverly Hills Police Department?"

I thought, because I wasn't until Quirk phoned Remington. I looked steadily at the Captain and asked, "Are you sure I didn't, Captain Apoyan?"

He frowned. "Of course I'm sure. We try to get along with all the departments in this area, Callahan."

"Glad to hear it," I said. "May I go now?"

Martin smiled. Pascal began to glare. Tommy said, "Take it easy now, Brock. Co-operation, that's the theme here."

I said nothing.

Martin nodded his head toward Apoyan and smiled at me. "This refugee from the rug business thinks you were working for me, Brock. That's what put you outside the pale."

Apoyan said hoarsely, "Watch your tongue, Martino."

Rick's attorney dug him with an elbow. "I guess we're all free to go now, aren't we, Captain?"

"Five seconds ago you were," Apoyan said. "But I won't take insolence from anyone. Perhaps your client and Mr. Callahan need a little cooling-off period."

Rick lighted a cigarette. I stood where I was, doing nothing.

Apoyan asked me, "Any further comment?"

I shook my head.

He looked at Martin.

Martin shook his head and smiled. He was richer than I was; he could afford the smile.

"All right," Apoyan said, "get out of here, all of you."

We went out quietly, giving him his moment. In the hall, Tommy said, "When are you going to lose your arrogance? When are you going to grow up?"

I didn't answer him. I said to Martin, "You must have had a good alibi for last night."

"Five of them," Martin said evenly. "I played cards until early this morning."

"With some pretty solid citizens, the way it looks."

He stared at me quizzically. "Solid enough. What's eating you, Callahan?"

The smile, I thought. Hoodlums smiling patronizingly at officers of the law. That will always eat me.

Tommy Self said, "As long as you interrupted my dinner, Brock. I'll let you buy me one."

I nodded.

Martin said, "You haven't answered my question, Callahan."

"Not now, Enrico," I told him. "Later, maybe I'll be able to."

I gave him my back and went out into the dusk with Tommy. "We'll take my car," I told Tommy. "Leave yours here."

"Yes, sir," Tommy mocked me. "Aren't *you* in a mood."

"I hate crooks," I said, "and I hate to be treated like one."

"You could be a coach, couldn't you? You've had offers from a couple of high schools, if I remember correctly."

"I don't want to be a coach."

"Well, if you insist on being a private eye, you'd better get used to this kind of treatment. You're nobody's friend."

"I'm not a private eye. I'm a private *investigator,* licensed by the Attorney General of the State of California."

"Oh, for Christ's sake, grow up!"

I stopped walking to glare at him. "Just exactly what did that mean?"

He didn't look awed. In all the years I've known him. I've never seen him awed or frightened. A perfect quarterback's attitude.

He said calmly, "I mean, get smart. Adjust. The people who come to you quite often have reasons why they can't take their troubles to the police. The police don't like that situation and the people who come to you are unhappy about it. You are going to have to be what they called you at Stanford, a rock. Impervious, immovable, invulnerable. That's the state of mind you'll have to develop. If you can't do that, get into coaching."

I put a fatherly hand on his shoulder. "You don't mean 'adjust,' Tommy. you mean 'surrender.' "

He sighed. "Who could ever get through to you? Even at school you used to check my signals, you, a lousy guard."

"I was the captain, Tommy," I reminded him gently. "I know it still burns the hell out of you, but *I* was the captain."

Silence, a miffed silence, from him. *I'm not a private eye,* I thought, *I'm a private I. I am what I am and it hasn't cost me too much yet, except for the lump on the head, the sore ribs, the puffed lip. And, of course, the bad knee.*

"Quit mumbling," Tommy said wearily. "That's another of your adolescent habits."

I opened the door of my car for him. "On your better days, kid, I think you were better than Frankie Albert."

"I never had a day when I wasn't better than Frankie," he said. "I'd like to eat at the Fox and Hounds."

I bought him a couple of drinks first and he mellowed. We ate twelve dollars' worth of food and I paid the tab, and he told me. "That's my fee for today."

"It's pretty high," I answered, "but I suppose not for a Harvard man."

I drove him back to his car and we parted friends. We really admired each other. We'd played in the days of two-platoon football, and Tommy and I were the only players to go both ways. Tommy was a little brighter and I was a lot bigger, so there was no reason for envy.

I watched him climb into his Cad and swung my Ford back toward Westwood.

There was another ache in me now, an ache for the tragedy of Jacqueline Held. She'd played a dangerous game, and lost. I wondered if Rick Martin had known about the Einlicher burried in the crisper drawer. I wondered who his card-playing alibis had been.

Other hoodlums? They'd swear on the Bible that the moon was green cheese and they'd eaten a piece of it. But no police officer would accept the word of a hoodlum. I hoped.

Of course, when a man reaches a certain financial eminence, he is no longer a hoodlum. He is one of the smart boys who made it. A rich man may be hated but he is rarely held in contempt.

Except by the private I's.

I is for Individual, I thought, *and where are they all, today?*

In my Westwood rattrap, a long, warm and soapy shower eased a few tensions. I is also for Investigator, and where did I go next? Up against Rick Martin? With what?

I is for Iconoclast and maybe I was wrong. Jan had often told me I was wrong and so had Tommy Self and both of them were bright and both successful in their respective trades.

My buzzer buzzed and I put a robe on before going to the door. Under the robe was only the brawny and muscular I.

Moira Quirk wore a sweater and skirt and a fingertip length, pale green cashmere jacket. Her perfume was delicate but disturbing.

"You didn't tell them about me," she said.

"Correct. Come in, Miss Quirk."

She came in and I closed the door. She looked around my dismal quarters and back at me. "You improve with knowing, Mr. Callahan."

"I'm a pretty fine guy," I admitted. "Won't you sit down? I don't drink that hard stuff myself, but I've got a bottle of vintage bourbon my aunt gave me for Christmas last year."

She went over to sit on my studio couch. "I could use a drink."

"All I'd have for it is water."

"If the whiskey is good enough, water is just right for it."

The whiskey was Old Forester, which should be good enough for anybody, any way. I poured a two-ounce shot of it into a glass, added water and ice and brought it to Miss Quirk.

The jacket was folded on the studio couch next to her, and she had lighted a cigarette. She took the glass I extended and thanked me. She said, "Why is it you don't drink? You're not still in training, are you?"

I shook my head. "I never cared for the flavor. About twice a year, when things pile up, I may go on a binge. But generally I stick to beer."

She rolled the glass in her hand. "Athletes—I mean, the good ones—seem so insufferably self—sufficient. Why is that?

"I don't know. It's a kind of physical arrogance that becomes mental after a while, I guess. Did you come here to talk about athletes, Miss Quirk?''

"*One* athlete," she said. "You may call me Moira. Would I call you Brock or the Rock? John used both, frequently."

"Brock will be fine. You came here to talk about Johnny?"

She nodded. She sipped her drink.

Slim she was, and undoubtedly scrubbed. High-bred and intelligent and faintly haughty. The challenge of conquest was heavy in the room and I was ashamed of my vulgar thoughts.

"What are you thinking?" she asked.

I smiled at her. "I'd rather not say."

An almost imperceptible color in her thin proud face. "Men will be men. And that's what I've been thinking about John."

"He kept busy," I agreed.

She nodded slowly. "And it's very possible that the more you dig into his background, the more—dirt you'll uncover."

I nodded. "Do you think I should quit digging?"

"Don't you?"

"If your father wants me to I will." I paused, and added, "Probably."

"Dad doesn't know what I know about John."

"Do you want to tell me what you know?"

"Nothing you probably don't. He seemed to have an—insatiable appetite for women, didn't he?"

"Most men have. But they aren't as lucky as Johnny was."

"That's cynical," she said.

"Yes, ma'am. Have you found another kind in your assault on the studios?"

"Very few. But studio people are hardly typical."

"No, they're luckier."

She sipped some more and considered me impersonally. "You expect nothing but the worst from people, don't you? That's what makes you invulnerable."

"Believe me, Moira, I'm far from invulnerable. But it doesn't follow that I must accept every Puritan myth. Johnny was as good and as bad as the next man, not much worse or better. In one field of endeavor, he was great. That makes him important and his death important to me."

"All right, *Rock*," She held up her glass. "Could I have some more of this?"

I had finished mixing it when my buzzer buzzed again. I took the drink with me to the door and opened it wide.

My beloved Jan stood there, looking penitent. "Friends?" she asked.

"Friends," I said.

She looked at the glass. "Whiskey? You?"

I shook my head. "Rarely touch it."

Then her glance took in the robe, and her eyes grew less soft. She pulled the robe back enough to see my bare leg. Her eyes were brown agates.

She looked around me and her face turned to stone. Moira was now in view.

"Come in, Jan," I said. "I've a client here who—"

My lady's voice was no more than a strangled whisper. "You dirty, slimy bastard. You—"

She was three steps away when I called, "Jan, listen to reason, will you? Jan, for heaven's sake—"

From the apartment next door Paul Kimball looked out to see what all the noise was about. He looked at Jan's retreating back, at my robed nakedness, at the drink in my hand. He sighed, shook his head, said, "These lucky bachelors," and sadly closed his door.

≈≈≈≈≈≈≈≈≈ *FOURTEEN* ≈≈≈≈≈≈≈≈≈

WHEN I TURNED around, Moira was smiling. "Who in the world was that?"

"Oh, she's sort of my girl. She misunderstood." I brought her her drink.

"Thank you. Did she— Do I know her?"

"You might. She's in business in Beverly Hills. Jan Bonnet is her name."

Moira nodded. "I've seen some of the houses she's done. Excellent taste, hasn't she?"

"I don't know. I'm more or less tasteless. Tell me, do you know Rick Martin personally?"

Her face was composed. "What made you think of him?"

"Jan knows him. I wondered how social he was in Beverly Hills."

Moira sipped her drink. "I've met him a few times. He knows quite a few studio people. That was a strange question, Brock Callahan."

"It's a strange case," I answered. "I wonder if it was Johnny who phoned Martin."

She didn't answer.

"It must have been," I said, "or why would Johnny be down there at the foot of the lot, waiting?"

Moira said quietly, "Because it was Thursday. Before my mother died, Thursday was her special day with John. And ever since then, when John was home, he went down there where she's buried. Whenever he got home, on a Thursday, just as he used to when he came home from school on Thursday." She took a deep breath and a deep swallow. "John had—he was inclined toward mysticism."

"Do you mean religion?"

"If that's your name for it. But you can see why I didn't want to tell the police that, don't you?"

I shook my head.

Her thin face was strained. "Can't you see the newspapers with quotes from some quack psychiatrist about the Oedipus complex and John's chasing after floozies? Don't you see the kind of freak they'd love to make of him? And you know John wasn't that."

I said nothing.

She finished her drink and stood up. "You made those drinks too strong. I'd better be going."

I held her coat for her, and her perfume was stronger. I said, "Even if I didn't continue to dig into Johnny's history, the police will."

She nodded quietly. "You were hired by my father, anyway. I couldn't call you off. Good luck, Brock."

"Good luck to you, Moira," I said gently. "Johnny was just like all the rest of us, a human being."

She turned around and kissed my cheek. Then she went quickly to the door and out, but not before I'd noticed her eyes were wet.

I thought of Jan, but that was painful, and I thought of Jackie Held. She must have known something she hadn't told us; I couldn't think of any other reason for her death. She was one of the minor temblors that follow an earthquake, a girl who'd edged too close to violence.

I wondered if she'd known who wrote the note that had been placed in Johnny's car. I wondered if she'd been in league with the killer. That last I couldn't accept.

I is for Impervious, Immovable and Invulnerable, which Tommy Self had told me I must be. I couldn't cut the mustard; I was none of these things, except on a good afternoon against a weak team. I was a rock in quicksand, sinking.

For some reason or other, people had always confided in me. But people in trouble are inclined to give you their side of the story. Johnny's side and Jackie's side were no longer available.

Go out into left field like Einstein, idiot guard. Pick up your theory from the stars and substantiate it with your mortal mind. Light flickered briefly in my dull and mortal mind—and went out.

I was physically, mentally, spiritually fatigued. I drank three glasses of water and went to bed.

By morning the wind had shifted, warming itself as it came down the slope of mountains into town. It was dry and hot and clear.

I ate at the drug store and went to the office. There I wrote a letter:

Dear Miss Bonnet:

Last evening I was taking a shower when my doorbell rang. I quickly put on a robe and went to the door. It was the daughter of my current client. She was emotionally disturbed and badly in need of a drink, which I furnished. If there had been anything wrong, would I have answered the door to your ring? I respectfully await your apology.

Hopefully,

B. Callahan

I addressed it to Jan at her shop address and dropped it in a collection box on the way to the police station.

Gnup wasn't there, but I got to see Lieutenant Remington. I asked him if they'd had any luck with the note Johnny had found in his car.

Remington shook his head. "Our only hope would be a new typewriter that went directly from factory to retailer to original buyer—and stayed there. Tracing a typewriter these days is almost impossible."

I said, "The Los Angeles boys will be in it now, since Miss Held was killed. That isn't going to hurt us."

Remington looked cynical. "I suppose they have more equipment, lab facilities."

"How about the bullet?" I asked.

He shook his head. "Too badly battered. It must have been a high-powered rifle, though. It went into that tree after going through Quirk's skull."

"You're sure the bullet you found in the tree was the same one that killed Johnny?"

Silence, and then Remington asked, "Have you some other theory, Callahan?"

"Not exactly. But we haven't gone very far with logic; maybe we could start over from scratch and get the theory first."

Remington said wearily, "Callahan, this is a police department, not a school for psychic research. We can't work by séance, you know, only by the methods that have proven to be most efficient through experience. Am I making myself clear?"

"Yes, sir. We're not doing so well, either, are we?"

"We're doing what we can," he said stiffly. "If you can think of a better policy, you are free to follow it."

"Yes, sir," I said. "Thank you, sir." I left him there glowering.

From my office, I phoned the West Los Angeles station and asked for Captain Apoyan. He wasn't there, so I asked for Sergeant Pascal, and got him.

"Any identifiable prints in Jackie Held's apartment?"

"Quite a few. Yours and Martino's among others."

"That figures," I said.

"I'm sure it will, eventually. Anything else?"

"Any prints you can't match up?"

"A few. We've sent them to Washington."

"Thanks, Sergeant," I said. "I'll keep in touch. Give my regards to Caroline."

The line went dead with a sharp click.

I was typing my reports when the door opened. A thin, tanned man in a cheap suit stood looking at me appraisingly. His white shirt wasn't quite and his bow tie was obviously on an elastic neckband.

"Howdy," he said. "Brock Callahan, right?"

"Right as rain, sir. Won't you come in?"

"Can't see why not." He tried to be casual, but was missing it. He came in and sat in my customer's chair, still studying me.

"You recongnized me," I said, "but I'm afraid I can't return the favor. Have we met?"

He shook his head and was silent, trying to look enigmatic.

That's what can happen to you from watching George Raft on TV.

I said, "You came as a prospective client?"

He shook his head again and permitted me a glimpse of a slight and knowing smile.

"What's your name?" I asked.

"Guess it doesn't matter. I live right close to where that Miss Held lives, *used* to live, that is."

"Oh? And you know something I should know?"

He had a chance for a pregnant line now and he gave it the full dramatic treatment. "Guess it would be better to say I know something you *do* know."

I said patiently, "Well, say it then, Mr. — ?"

"I saw you there yesterday. I saw the girl you talked to for so long, the girl in the Lincoln convert."

I was getting his pitch now. I said easily, "Pretty girl, wasn't she?"

He nodded, watching me warily. "Read the paper this morning. Nothing in the paper about the girl."

"Her press agent isn't as good as he should be. What are you trying to tell me, Mr. — ?"

"Call me Jones, if you hanker after a name," he said. "Things are rough these days, with taxes and all."

I leaned back in my chair and frowned at him. "Are you trying to blackmail me, Mr. Jones?"

A silence, while he reddened.

"Why didn't you take this information to the police, Mr. Jones?"

"I'm not looking to give anybody trouble," he said. "I'm looking to help where I can."

"I see. Do you watch *all* the neighbors?"

His redness grew. "I'm no snooper. I just happened to be looking out the window and I saw what I saw, is all."

"And you brought it to me," I said quietly. "Anything else you could tell me about Miss Held, Mr. Jones?"

"That sports car used to be parked there plenty often. That one young Quirk drove. And there was an Imperial there plenty, too."

"Any others?"

"Not regular. None I noticed more than once."

"But some you noticed once. What kind of cars were they?"

"I don't recollect."

Silence, while he fought to get back to dominance and I fought to keep my temper. He was too small to hit and too poor to insult.

After a moment I asked, "Are you in a hurry, Mr. Jones?"

He looked at me suspiciously. "I don't get you."

"I'll talk to the girl who owns the Lincoln. If she wants to pay to avoid unpleasant publicity, I'll let you know. Could I have your right name?"

He shook his head and stood up to smile down at me. "I'll keep in touch with you, Mr. Callahan. I'll just be Jones, when I call."

I watched him walk out and thought, *You'll always just be Jones*. People get the damnedest ideas, watching television.

I went to the window and waited for him to come out from the building below. He came out, looked both ways along the sidewalk, but didn't look up toward me. He climbed into a prewar Plymouth parked a few spaces up, not too far for me to make out the license number. I wrote the number down to incorporate into my report later.

It was eleven when I finished typing, too early for lunch and too late to go any place before lunch. I sat and tried to think.

I examined the death of Jackie Held from every available angle. She had been a friend of Martin's, of the Heffner's and of Johnny Quirk. Had she also been a confidante, and how much of one?

Johnny, I had learned, revealed different parts of his complex personality to oddly various people. Had he told her something he hadn't told the others? Or had she learned something since his death that made her existence dangerous to the killer?

It was logical to assume their deaths were connected; the coincidence would be too big to swallow, otherwise.

I ran the list of characters over in my mind; going back over the cycle seemed futile and pointless. I would have to find a new list of suspects, or go after the old ones from a new angle.

I picked up the phone and called Moira Quirk.

≋≋≋≋≋≋≋≋≋≋≋≋*FIFTEEN*≋≋≋≋≋≋≋≋≋≋≋≋≋

MR. BROCKTON'S DESK was near a window and he sat with his back to it. On the wall at one side of the window was a portrait of George Washington. On the wall at the other side was a portrait of Abraham Lincoln.

Mr. Brockton's face was lower than these and directly between them and he undoubtedly suffered from the proximity. His face was too soft, too white and too undistinguished. He looked like what he was, a high school principal.

He said worriedly, "I can't see that anything worthwhile can result from investigating a sordid incident in our school's past, Mr. Callahan. It certainly will add no luster to the reputation of the deceased. He was a fine boy, Mr. Callahan, in many ways. He was forthright and energetic and sensitive."

"I know, Mr. Brockton," I said humbly. "Knowing that is what keeps me working on the case."

His gray eyes searched me. "Are you sure? Or are you simply seeking more sensationalism for this already over-publicized tragedy?"

"I'm an investigator, not a reporter, Mr. Brockton."

Silence in the room. Washington looked down at me austerely and Lincoln sadly. Mr. Brockton looked beyond me, perhaps reliving this "sordid incident in our school's past."

Finally he sighed. "Her name was Miss Elinore Arness. I've no idea where she is now, or whether she's teaching or not."

"She left here immediately after the incident, of course."

His eyes widened. "Of course."

"Would you still have the address she lived at while she was employed here?"

"We might. If you'll excuse me a moment?" He rose and went into the outer office.

I thought Lincoln smiled at me, but Washington's expression didn't change. I heard the clack of a typewriter through the open door and then the sound stopped. There was a murmur of low voices.

The whole building seemed unnaturally quiet, though the fall term had commenced. It must be a well-disciplined school and I could guess at the shock Miss Arness' indiscretion must have caused.

Mr. Brockton came in with a file card and handed it to me.

I thanked him and went down the quiet corridor, disturbed only by the soft voices of the explaining teachers. The address was a West Los Angeles address; most teachers can't afford to live in Beverly Hills.

It was a six-unit structure of stucco on three sides and red-wood on the front side. The owner-manager lived in Apartment One.

He was a fat man in dungarees and a faded Hawaiian sport shirt. "Miss Elinore Arness?" he said, and his smile was obscene. "She left town right after that mess she got into. Moved to Phoenix. That's in Arizona, you know."

"I've heard of it," I said modestly. "Do you have a forwarding address for her?"

"The missus might. You a collector or something?"

"A producer," I told him. "I think she'd make an interesting movie."

He looked at me knowingly. "For stags, you mean?"

I winked at him. "See if the missus has the address, huh?"

He went inside and I heard him ask, "You got that Arness woman's Phoenix address?"

"So what if I have? Who wants it?"

Silence and then his voice was gruffer. "C'mon, don't get smart. You been writing to her, ain't you?"

"There's a law against it? Who wants her address?"

Silence again, and then, "I'll give you ten seconds."

Silence, the shuffle of feet, and he said, "Some day, Alice — pow!" He chuckled.

He came to the door and handed me an address torn off an envelope. He said, "The missus has been writing her."

Through the open doorway I could see the missus dimly.

She couldn't have been much under two hundred pounds. I thanked him and went down to the car.

In Westwood I had the oil drained and had them put in a new cleaner cartridge with the refill. I had the gas tank filled and the radiator flushed and refilled, and it was three o'clock.

That was all right. I wouldn't get to the desert until the heat of the day was waning. Driving throught the desert is done best at night, in September, but it wouldn't be too bad by the time I got there.

I got onto the freeway in Hollywood, and headed for Highway 60-70.

I thought back to Sunday night, and Jackie asleep on the davenport, full of Scotch. It didn't figure that she would top that off with beer. Unless, of course, she'd run out of Scotch and wakened with the thirst. Or unless she had eaten after I had left and the beer had seemed to fit the meal. Like with enchiladas. Or her visitor might have taken her out for dinner, or brought some food over. And who knew *when* the conine had gone into the beer? I shivered, remembering that I'd had two bottles of it.

When I'd first met Jackie, she hadn't wanted to admit she knew any gamblers. Was that to protect Rick Martin? Or the Heffners?

I ran the flivver up to sixty miles an hour when I got into the open country. Cars went by me like I was parked. Big cars, little cars, old cars and new ones, killers licensed by the state. I kept as far to the right as possible and went up to seventy.

It grew hotter as I approached Riverside, and the traffic was as its worst right now. But I still wasn't hungry; I drove on, into the desert.

A single lane on each side of the white line now, and the cars coming toward me were driving directly into that blinding sun. I tried not to think of them. In the distance the mountains were purple and serene, the shimmer of heat waves danced lazily across the limitless, cactus-studded plain.

This had probably been a sea before man appeared. I wondered if it would ever be a sea again when man had finally managed to exterminate himself. Every few miles there was a culvert over a sun-baked arroyo, and at every culvert there were a few trees. Perhaps in the rainy season those arroyos were flooded, but where did the trees get their moisture now?

Only a few miles beyond Indio I saw what I thought must be a mirage. A whiskered, lath-thin prospector was plodding along not twenty feet off the road, heading toward Indio, his burro plodding patiently behind him.

Neither the burro nor the man seemed to notice the high speed traffic of the highway; both of them seemed lost in thoughts of a quieter, better time.

At Blythe, I ate. Blythe could have been put up by the California Chamber of Commerce—a green oasis on the California side of the Colorado River. A traveler from the East is startled when he leaves the gray of the Arizona desert as he crosses the bridge into Blythe. After Blythe, on the west, the desert starts again. But that first glimpse of green after countless miles of desert driving is like land to a shipwrecked mariner.

The sun was only a red ball on the western horizon now, but the temperture was still well over a hundred in Blythe. The cafe was air-conditioned and seemed chilly and dim after the glare of the road.

I ordered a chicken in a basket and a bottle of beer and went into the washroom to bathe my dry and drawn face. The lip was going down, and so was the bump; my hand no longer ached.

The beer was cold, the chicken falling off the bone. The waitress told me today hadn't been so bad, but yesterday had run up to a hundred and fourteen. It was an unseasonable September.

By the time I got to Quartzite it was completely dark. At Wickenburg the road turned south, toward Phoenix. I gassed up there.

I was down to forty miles an hour now. I was going to get into town too late to go calling, anyway, and there is always an empty motel room in Phoenix in September.

Los Angeles is not the West in the true sense. A man has to get out of town to see the West, the desert and the mountains and the quiet sea. Phoenix, too, is not the West. Phoenix is a collection of automobile agencies and motels and memories, a drab and dusty town in the middle of a dull and dusty plain.

The summer rates were still in effect; I got a motel room with a small kitchenette for five dollars. There was air conditioning and a forty-foot pool.

I showered and changed my shirt and drove out to the north end of town to the address the fat man had given me. It was an old frame house on a half-acre of ground, a worn house but rich with foliage and flowers. There was no light showing, and I drove back to the motel.

Water ran through the irrigation ditches along the road; the banked lawns were being flooded. In Phoenix, water for growing things is rationed and tap water is too expensive for irrigation.

In my motel room the heat of the day still held. I turned on the cooler and sat up for a while before going to bed.

Elinore Arness had taught English at that high school. According to Mr. Brockton, she was a very attractive woman and had been on the sunny side of thirty when involved with Johnny. I went to sleep framing words for Miss Arness in my mind.

In the morning I had breakfast at a dining room two motels up the road. The sun was well up and the pool beckoned, but I dutifully climbed into the hot flivver and drove to the Arness domain.

A sun-bleached station wagon with one crumpled fender was parked on the gravel driveway. The wagon bore New Mexico plates. The garage door was open and a thin and swarthy young man was in there mixing paint. He wore jeans and high-heeled cowboy boots and no shirt.

He looked up as I parked, and came over, wiping his hands on a rag, as I stepped from the flivver.

He was handsome in a weak and oily way and I could guess he would appear attractive to women. I said, "I'm looking for Miss Elinore Arness."

Arrogance was plain on his sensitive face. "Why?"

"Why not?" I asked.

He couldn't have weighed more than a hundred and sixty or so, but he was a full inch taller than I am and my weight didn't seem to register on him at all.

"Beat it," he said.

"Easy, now. It's Miss Arness I came to see, not you. Let

her decide whether she wants to talk to me or not.''

His narrow face showed no emotion. "You're trespassing. I could run in and get a gun, or I could carve you up." His hand went into his jeans pocket and came out with a knife. A click, and the long narrow blade flashed in the bright Arizona sun.

"I could go into town and get a police officer," I said, "or I could make you eat that knife. Don't mess with me, punk; I'm here to see Miss Elinore Arness."

"You're trespassing," he said again.

"On *your* property?"

"I watch it during the day, when Miss Arness is gone. And she particularly doesn't like people from California."

There was no quaver in his voice and no quiver I could see in his body. I think he wanted me to make a move toward him. The knife was held low, ready to slash up, and he probably knew how to use it.

I asked quietly, "Where or how can I reach Miss Arness?"

He shook his head. "There's no way. Haven't you bastards bothered her enough?"

"What bastards?"

He looked at me calmly. "You're trespassing. That's the last warning."

"I'll be back," I told him. "Don't go away."

He smiled. "I'll be here."

Across the road and about a hundred feet down it, a woman with pruning shears had stood watching us from the front yard of her new ranch house. I drove over there.

She was a tanned woman on the hopeful side of forty, and she gave her attention to a grapefruit tree as I parked in front. When the door of my car slammed, she looked up.

I gave her one of the business cards that mentioned the credit side of my many-faceted agency and told her, "I'm trying to locate Miss Elinore Arness. I ran into a little difficulty across the street."

Her light blue eyes searched my face as she nodded. "I thought I saw a knife in his hand. Was I right?"

I nodded. "One of the perils of the trade. Could you tell me where I could find Miss Arness now?"

She continued to study me. "I like Elinore. I like her a lot. Her taste in men puzzles me, but I guess none of us are perfect, are we?"

"None I've met," I said. "Don't you want to tell me where she works?"

"I'm not sure," she said, "Would you like a glass of grapefruit punch? It's a hot day."

I smiled. "I'm not one to belittle the mañana attitude, but I'm here on business."

She smiled in return. "I know. I saw the plates on your car. If you're not in too much of a hurry, we could sit on the porch and have some punch and I could decide what I want to tell you."

I looked up the road to the next house doubtfully.

The woman said, "They don't know anything about Elinore. They only recently moved here. Well, I guess I'm taking up your time." She started for the house.

"Wait," I said. "I'm thirsty for grapefruit punch."

It was a narrow porch, running the whole length of the house. I sat in a rattan rocker and waited. I thought I heard a voice from inside the house and wondered if the woman was on the phone. I hadn't heard it ring.

Across the street the slim young man was painting the garage a pastel yellow. High in the sky beyond the house a buzzard circled and dipped. On the dry Bermuda grass of the front lawn the clippings were already wilting and curling in that hot sun. Footsteps, and my hostess came out the front door carrying a dewy pitcher and a pair of tumblers stenciled in a cowboy motif.

The stuff was pink, for some reason. But tart and tasty. We sipped, and watched the thin man paint the garage.

"Cigarette?" my hostess asked, and offered a white box of English cigarettes.

"No, thank you. Miss Arness never married?"

"No. What store in Los Angeles wants a credit report on her?"

"None that I know of. Credit investigations are only part of my work."

The delicate odor of mild tobacco came to me and I looked over to see my hostess staring fixedly at the man painting.

I said, "Do you know Elinore Arness very well?"

She continued to look at the painter. "I guess I'm her best friend in Phoenix."

"Perhaps you can guess why I'm here."

"Perhaps. Juan was in Los Angeles at the time—that Quirk boy died."

"Juan? Oh, you mean the man who's painting the garage now?"

"That's the man, Juan Duarez. Do you like Mexicans?"

"Nationalities have no meaning to me. Don't you?"

She expelled her breath. "I'm afraid not. And I guess that's bigotry. I was born in this town."

I said nothing.

My hostess went on quietly. "When Elinore first moved here, she did quite a bit of drinking. That's how I happened to learn the story of this Quirk boy. And then I read about his murder and now you're here and I can guess you're not here for a credit check, and I'm wondering why you are here." She was facing me.

"On a very wild hunch," I said. "I thought she might have a knowledge of Johhny's history that would help me to trap his killer. I wasn't getting anywhere on that suspect merry-go-round in Los Angeles, so I came here to back a wild hunch."

"Is Juan Duarez the wild hunch?"

"No. I never heard of him until you told me his name."

"Isn't he awful? He lives with her. I haven't seen much of Elinore since he moved in."

I didn't answer.

"More punch?" she asked.

"No, thank you, though it was delicious. Do you want to tell me now where I can find Miss Arness?"

The woman stood up. "There's no reason why I shouldn't, I suppose. Her business address is in the phone book under her name. Don't you investigators ever look up addresses in the phone book?"

"Only the experienced investigators, ma'am," I said humbly.

SIXTEEN

It was a small shop on a quiet side street downtown. The lettering on the window informed me that "The Bay" was ready to supply me with stationary, greeting cards, magazine subscriptions, new and used typewriters and the services of a rental library.

The natural blonde who sat at the small desk in the rear of the shop was slim and tall and would have been considered willowy except for an exceptional bust development.

Her smile was pale and her "Good morning" was delivered in a refined and pleasing voice. She stood up and I saw her long, fine legs. She came closer and I saw her very delicate coloring.

"Miss Arness?" I asked, and she frowned slightly, but nodded.

"My name is Brock Callahan," I said. "I'm—"

"Are you the man who was out at the house?" she asked. "Are you the man who threatened Juan?"

I shook my head. "I'm the man Juan threatened. I come as a friend, Miss Arness."

Her voice was soft but tense. "Please leave, Mr. Callahan. Juan is sure you could be jailed for trespassing, but I don't want any trouble. Please leave now."

"You could have a lot of trouble, getting your legal advice from Juan," I told her. "Johnny Quirk came to me for help before he died, Miss Arness."

Her voice was higher. "Please go. *Please!*"

Her face had blanched to a whiteness that unnerved me. She seemed poised on the rim of hysteria. I turned around, and walked out.

Across the street there was a coffee shop, and though I didn't want any coffee, the front tables in the place were excellent vantage points. I went over to toy with a milk shake.

Nothing happened. A few people, obviously customers, went into the Bay and came out carrying books or packages. Juan Duarez didn't put in an appearance; he was probably still painting the garage.

Maybe he hadn't been the one who'd phoned Elinore Arness; perhaps the tanned neighbor had performed that chore. I thought of the neighbor and compared her to the pale elegance of Miss Arness. How could a girl keep that complexion in this climate?

Miss Arness had that inbred British look—but at the same time motherly. Her impressive mammary development would be the major appeal to a lad with an Oedipus complex. They can never seem to get weaned.

Vulgar thoughts about a lovely lady; there was a bad taste in my mouth and it wasn't from the milk shake. But to continue, what had Johnny had that attracted her?

More than Juan Duarez, certainly, I told myself, and who can understand a woman's taste in men? Or a man's taste in women? At fifteen, Johnny had undoubtedly tired of the budding promises under the unnecessary brassières of his classmates. I know I had.

I paid for the milk shake and walked over to a haberdashery and bought a pair of cheap swimming trunks. I drove back to the motel and used the pool. The chances seemed to be good that I'd get nowhere here, but I wasn't doing any better in Los Angeles.

I continued to think of the tanned and friendly neighbor. After my shower I bought a quart of ice cream and two orders of barbecued chicken and drove back there.

The station wagon wasn't on the drive of the Arness place when I went past. One wall of the garage was painted and the garage door was closed.

My tanned friend came to the door with an apron on. She looked quizzically at the packages. "Migawd, now what?"

"Barbecued chicken and ice cream for two," I told her. "I suppose it's presumptuous of me, but you seemed so friendly . . ."

A pause, while she studied me. "Are you on the make or something, young man?"

"I'm not so young," I said. "My mistake, huh?"

"Come in," she said. "I'm just putting the coffee on."

I came into a large, beamed living room with adobe walls and through a fair-sized dining room to a real ranch kitchen. There, she sniffed the chicken and said, "Needs a little warming." She opened an oven door that led directly into the adobe wall.

"The Betty Furness of the West," I said. "You've really fixed yourself up, haven't you?"

"And for what?" she asked me. "You don't have any friends a few years older, do you?"

"You wouldn't want a man any older than I am."

She turned to look at me. "I want a man around forty. I'm thirty-seven."

I grinned at her. "I'll screen my friends when I get home. Weren't you ever married?"

She nodded. "Once. To a man considerably older. He died two years ago and left me one small oil well. It'll never make me rich, but it just keeps pumping along."

Her name was Bella, Bella Carruthers, and she told me about her twenty years with the late Sam Carruthers. Sam had tried everything that wasn't tied to a time clock, from oil painting to oil prospecting, and had been killed by an oil casting that erupted when his first big one came in.

I told her I shared her late husband's aversion to working for somebody else, and couldn't we go into the living room with our coffee? I wanted to watch the house across the street.

She sniffed. "I see the light, finally. All right."

The station wagon was nowhere in sight; the garage door was still closed. I asked Bella, "Did you see him drive away?"

"No. I was working in the back yard."

"Did you phone Miss Arness and tell her about me?"

A pause, and she nodded. "She's still my friend, you know."

"I know. Tell me about her."

"She's highly emotional, at times. She's very well read. She was an English teacher, you know."

I nodded. "When did this Duarez move in?"

"About a month ago. He came into the store asking for work. He said he wanted to be around books. Some line, eh?"

"Maybe. And she didn't want him in the store?"

"Not in Phoenix. Her customers would prefer getting their literary recommendations from her. But there was work for a man around her house, and here was this seeking mind, you see, thirsty as a new blotter, and—"

"And young and handsome," I finished for her. "And here was this extra bedroom, and history about to repeat itself."

"Let's try not to be nasty," Bella said quietly.

"I'm trying. I suppose I could go over there with a bottle tonight."

"If you were a real son-of-a-bitch you could. Elinore didn't join the A.A.; she cured herself. A man would need to be some bastard to put her back on that toboggan."

"I've been called worse, Bella."

Silence in the beamed living room. I turned around to see Bella glaring bleakly out into space. I said, "I wouldn't be that much of a bastard."

She took a deep breath. "I wasn't thinking of that. I was thinking of the month after Sam died. I really hit the bottle that month. It's easy to go down that road, isn't it?"

"I guess." I finished my coffee. "Juan said something about all the bastards having bothered her enough. What did he mean by that?"

"I don't know. Maybe he meant reporters. They gave her a bad time in Los Angeles when that mess broke."

"Maybe he thought I was a reporter. I'll bet that's it."

Nothing from Bella.

"I wonder what Juan's history is," I said musingly.

Bella sipped her coffee. "It could be very innocent. Your trade has made you suspicious and my heritage has made me bigoted, but he might be a real nice boy."

"A real nice boy with a sharp knife," I added. "I suppose I'm keeping you from something?"

She shook her head and stared at me quietly. "Mr. Callahan, you don't intend any harm for Elinore, do you? You're going to be very tactful if you talk to her, aren't you?"

"I mean her no harm. All I want is some information for a crazy theory."

"All right, I'll phone her." Bella stood up. "Maybe she could meet you here, tonight, after she closes the shop. Juan wouldn't bother you here."

"I'd appreciate that," I said. "Assure her I'm no scandal-monger."

I didn't get all of her dialogue with Elinore Arness, but she seemed to be making progress. When she came back to the living room she told me, "I think it's going to be all right. Could I phone you at your motel?"

I told her she could, and that I'd be waiting. I looked up the phone number of the Bide A While Motel and wrote it on the back of my business card.

Then I went back to the swimming pool to bide a while. When I began to turn red over my tan, I moved over into the shade with a two-bit book.

I'd rather read *anything* than read nothing; I read on. The sun stayed as hot, but continued toward the west. Some teenage girls in skimpy suits drove up; probably friends of the manager's daughter. I watched them cavort in my elderly and licentious way and thought of all the girls I'd known in high school and cursed myself for all the opportunities I had undoubtedly over-looked in my adolescent urge to be a nine-letter man.

My almost unblemished morality hadn't been the result of self-discipline; it had resulted from my following the more important urge toward a school athletic record.

Johnny, too, had been a nine-letter man, but his extracurricu-lar activities had gone far beyond the scope of the playing field, all the way to involement with the faculty. Had he died because of that? It could very well be.

The teenagers went away in a squeal of farewells and the water in the pool became placid. The afterwork traffic had diminished and I went to my room to check my watch. It was six o'clock.

The stationery store should be closing now; I would soon hear from Bella Carruthers.

At 6:45, I was in the manager's office, explaining about the

importance of the call I might get while I was out eating dinner
I hadn't finished when the phone rang, and it was for me.

Bella said, "Juan will be going to school tonight. Elinore
will see you at home, after seven o'clock."

"Thanks, Bella," I said. "You've been a real friend, to
both of us."

"Remember that when you get back to L.A., Callahan. And
send me someone serviceable."

I ate at the motel up the road again and I ate lightly. I arrived
in front of the Arness place about seven-twenty. The station
wagon wasn't in sight, but there was a Studebaker Champion
parked in front of the garage.

The sun was only a red glow over the mountains; there was
just enough light for me to see Bella in her back yard. She
waved as I got out of the car and I waved back.

I was nervous, for some reason, walking up to the front door
of Elinore Arness' home. I had visions of a lad with a knife
lurking behind the shrubs that bordered the house.

Miss Elinore Arness was in a powder-blue dress of some
filmy material and her house was a blend of pastels, pale and
cool. She sat on a light gray love seat; I sat on a light green chair.

"I wanted to know about Johnny and his friends," I told
her. "And about Moira Quirk. Did she go to Beverly Hills
High School, too?"

Elinore Arness told me about Johnny and his friends. She'd
been the faculty adviser for the school paper and had founded
its literary discussion group. She had been, if one accepted all
her claims as true, the real cultural center of Beverly Hills High
School during her time there. She'd been a student favorite.

She avoided discussion of the "incident" unless I asked her
direct questions about it. I asked her several, and the color rose
in her cheeks and her voice grew tighter, but she answered me
fully and, I hoped, honestly.

I didn't need to prompt her very often; I seemed to have
triggered a storehouse full of reminiscences that had been in
the dark too long.

She talked on and on and I waited patiently for additional
items to buttress my case.

When she'd finally run out of memories, it was almost nine

o'clock. I thanked her and told her she'd been a great help. At the door I asked her, "Do you know that Juan carries a switch knife?"

She nodded. "Is that his sin, or society's?"

"I don't know. The knife is Juan's and the attitude is society's, I suppose. I thought you could do something constructive about the knife."

Elinore Arness sighed. "Time, Mr. Callahan—it takes time to change an attitude."

I didn't argue with her. The first job, from my pedestrian viewpoint, would be to take away the knife and then work on the attitude. I thanked her again and went down to the car.

It was dark, and I could see the lights in Bella Carruther's cozy fortress and I contemplated going over there for a cup of coffee. But I decided against it. That desert would be murder tomorrow; I'd drive back to Los Angeles tonight.

Going back to the motel, I thought of a seed for murder, planted years ago and being nourished by envy and watered by hate. A case I had for my own mind, but not for a court of law. Facts, facts, facts, where were the facts, as Sergeant Friday would say.

I saw the station wagon just before I turned into the motel driveway. It was parked across the street.

The night air was cooler than the day had been, but not enough to give me a chill. I stopped at the office to tell the manager I was checking out, and tried to case the whole parking area while he prepared a bill for my expense account.

I was brushing my teeth when there was a knock on the door.

≋≋≋≋≋≋≋≋ *SEVENTEEN* ≋≋≋≋≋≋≋≋

I OPENED THE door and Juan said, "I told you to leave her alone."

I looked at him steadily. "Come in, Juan. I'm just getting ready to leave." I turned my back on him and returned to the bathroom.

When I came out of the bathroom Juan stood near the doorway and the door was closed.

"Gringo," he said.

I nodded. "Miss Arness, too. She helped me to search for a killer. You can believe that Miss Arness' first concern would be with justice, wouldn't you? And tracking down a killer is that."

"I told you to leave her alone."

"I know you did. But you're not my boss, Juan. I'll never see her again, probably. Don't threaten me."

He stood with his back to the door, both hands empty. I wondered how long they'd stay empty. I said quietly, "I'm leaving now. I'm not coming back."

His face was doubtful, for a change. "You're not coming back?"

I smiled. "I'll make a deal with you. You give me that knife in your pocket, and I'll never see you again."

He stared at me, still doubtful.

I said gently, "Hasn't Miss Arness got enough trouble? Can a knife bring her anything but more trouble?"

He took a deep and labored breath. "Gringo talk."

"That's right. And you've decided to live in a gringo world. Well, I'm going, whether you give me the knife or not." I moved toward the door.

He paused and stepped aside.

He was next to me when I opened the door; he was behind me when I went through it. My shoulder blades hunched but I resisted the impulse to turn around.

Five steps past the doorway I heard his "Wait, Mr. Callahan."

I turned and waited.

His hand was in his pocket now, and it came out holding the knife. But there was no click this time. He came over to give it to me.

"Thanks, amigo," I said, "and good luck. Look me up if you ever get into Los Angeles."

He smiled for the first time in our acquaintanceship. He nodded.

He was still standing in the parking area when I drove away, heading west.

The stars were out and there was a three-quarter moon. The flivver was full of gas and talking quietly to herself. My mind wasn't in the here and now, it was back in Beverly Hills High School some years ago.

Miss Arness was a perceptive woman. She'd been all teacher, before and after the school bell, and she had a sound memory. She'd filled me in exceptionally well on the roster of names I'd given her.

We can't always prove what we believe. Particularly to a judge or a jury of our peers.

I wondered if Juan Duarez had ever gone to high school. I should have asked him. I wondered what had happened in town during my absence and if they had buried Jackie Held and where.

Lights from approaching cars flickered in the clear desert air and took minutes to reach me across the flat wasteland. This is the way the world ends, this is the way the world ends, this . . .

I would need some coffee somewhere along the route.

Not with a bang but a whimper. Who were the whimperers in this case? Not Moira nor Pascal nor the Heffners. Mr. Quirk could be a whimperer, and Elinore Arness, and Sergeant Gnup had the attributes, bluster though he did.

In the police laboratories trained men could fashion a case sound enough for a prosecutor to take into court. When amateurs commit premeditated murder, they are inclined to leave clues because they try to weave a pattern of misdirection to cover the murder. And once the pattern is clear, the murderer is found. Though not necessarily tried. That takes the facts, ma'am.

There was a cafe open in Blythe, and a gas station. I drank three cups of coffee and brought the tank back to full again, though I'd only used six gallons to come from Phoenix.

Indio, flat and unimpressive. Beaumont. At Riverside, I cut over to the new road. The night air was colder, now; I kept one of the vents partly open to refresh my fuzzy mind.

It was almost six o'clock when I finally pulled up in front of my Westwood wigwam. I left the car in front and went up and right into the hay.

By noon I had had only six hours' sleep, but I knew it would be a waste of time to court more. I showered and shaved and picked up the *Times* from outside my apartment door.

The murder had arrived at page seven. Nothing, nothing, nothing, though the writer tried to hint at imminent disclosures.

I drank three glasses of warm milk and drove over to the Beverly Hills Police Station.

Lieutenant Remington was spending the day in Palm Springs, but Gnup was present and glowering.

"Where the hell you been?" he wanted to know.

"Phoenix. Were you looking for me, Sergeant?"

He nodded. "Why didn't you tell us about Halvorsen?"

"Because I don't know any Halvorsen."

Gnup's stare was ominous. "Don't lie. He came to you."

"Not under that name. Do you mean the man who lived near Jackie Held?"

"That's the one. He tried to blackmail Miss Quirk. She came to us, like a citizen should."

I smiled. "A *Beverly Hills* citizen, you mean, Sergeant. I didn't come to you because I wasn't sure how good Miss Quirk's credit was down here."

His voice was low. "Watch it, Callahan."

I said mildly, "I'm sorry, Sergeant. A man who called himself Jones came to see me just before I left for Phoenix. I didn't think he was important enough to demand immediate attention.

I put his call and license number into my report for that day and my files are always open to the department.''

He lighted a cigarette and shook his head. "You've always got an answer, haven't you? Why did you go to Phoenix?"

"To try and substantiate a random guess."

He looked interested. "What'd you come up with?"

"Enough." I paused. "Sergeant, if I told you what I think, you might go bulling in and lose us a murderer. I mean that as no criticism; it's standard police procedure. I'm not ready for the police yet. I haven't got all the information I want."

His soft mouth twisted into a snarl. "You've already withheld information from us, Callahan. Don't put yourself any deeper into the hole."

I said earnestly, "Sergeant, I came here this afternoon because I'm working with you. But I want a little more time; I want to do this right. Did you get that fingerprint report from Washington?"

He shook his head. "Not yet. Have you got somebody in mind we should print?"

"I might have, some time tonight. Will Lieutenant Remington be back tonight?"

He nodded. "I can phone him right now if you want him here."

I put a hand on Gnup's shoulder. "He doesn't need the ink. You can have it, Sergeant, I'll keep in touch." I started to walk out.

"Just a second, wise guy," he said.

I turned and waited.

His eyes were suspicious. "You're not playing it cute with me?"

"Me?" I shook my head sadly. "Sergeant, I'm in business in this town. I'm a rock, incorruptible. You know me and my reputation."

He snorted. "I'm learning more about both every day. You cross me, Callahan, and you'll wish you were dead."

"Fair enough, Sergeant. I'll phone you later."

I drove from there to the office and typed up the report of my Phoenix trip. I ate a ham sandwich at the drug store and drove over to the Quirk home.

Mr. Quirk was out for a drive with the chauffeur; the maid didn't know where Miss Moira was. I drove over to the Curtis place.

Pat was at home, working on the Ferrari. He told me he thought Deborah was going to be all right; she was in Pasadena for the day.

I asked him, "Were you the best shot in the Beverly Rifle Club?"

He hadn't been but he told me who had been.

I asked him if he remembered any others of the local gang who had been at the Orleans Room that night. He couldn't remember that any of the others had been there.

His eyes were shadowed. "Don't you think this is a gang kill, Mr. Callahan?"

"What gang?"

"You know what I mean. Gamblers, hoodlums."

"What do you think?" I asked him.

His tone was faintly belligerent. "What else could it be?"

"I'm not sure. Johnny must have had other enemies. There must have been plenty of boys who loved your sister. And still do."

"That doesn't mean they'd kill."

"Pat, different people do things for different reasons. Some men will kill you simply because they don't like the way you think. And men have been killed for half a bottle of cheap wine; I've seen the corpses and the killers. Life is very unimportant to some people."

"Not to me," he said. "Why are you here, Mr. Callahan?"

"For information only, boy," I told him. "Be good."

I left him and drove over to where Twentieth Century-Fox cast its huge shadow.

The home of Einar Halvorsen, née Jones, was almost directly across the street from the triplex. Einar came to the door in person to glare at me.

"I was in Phoenix," I explained. "You shouldn't have been so impatient."

"Get out of here," he said.

"Don't get smart, Halvorsen. Miss Quirk was decent enough not to press charges, but it's still not too late."

"Why are you bothering me?"

"I thought you might have noticed the car of the man who visited Miss Held late Sunday night. The police would be very grateful to a man who had noticed that."

He said grudgingly, "I'd like to help. But I went right to bed after church Sunday night and didn't wake up once."

"Well, perhaps you've noticed the car before. It's a green '53 Ford Club Coupe with whitewall tires."

He shook his head. "Doesn't register with me. That flivver of yours is the only Ford I ever noticed there. That dame had rich friends."

"Mr. Halvorsen," I said grimly, "the police still resent the fact that Miss Quirk wouldn't let them prosecute you. Now could be a good time to make yourself a hero."

He shook his head again. "Believe me, Mr. Callahan, I want to help and would if I could. But I never noticed any Ford over there except yours."

So I had nothing solid. There were some fingerprints and a typewritten note, but maybe the fingerprints would prove valueless and the typewriter might never be found. I had accusations to make and a rather logical theory in my mind, but the district attorney would want more than that.

I went back to the office to sulk.

A little after five, my phone rang and it was Moira Quirk. The maid had told her I'd called.

"I had some questions to ask you, Moira," I told her, "but Pat Curtis answered them for me. I gave you bad advice about that Halvorsen person, didn't I?"

"You meant well. Where have you been?"

"In Phoenix."

A fairly long silence, and then, "Oh?"

"I went to see Miss Arness."

"Why, Brock?"

"The case seemed to lead there. She's in business in Phoenix now."

Another silence, and, "Do you remember what we talked about at your place that night? Do you see what I mean now? Wouldn't the newspapers love to know you went to Phoenix?"

"They won't learn it from me. Moira, we have laws in this country. They were originally designed to see that justice is done. Clever and influential people occasionally circumvent the original purpose of those laws. But you don't want to be that kind of person, do you?"

"No. Of course not. If I thought you would find the person that killed John, I wouldn't care how many family skeletons were exposed. But I'd hate to think they were exposed in vain."

"I've got a lead, a strong one. Now, all I need is documentation. Is your father back from his drive?"

"Yes, but he's resting. He's—not himself at all; I think it would be better not to disturb him."

"All right. I'll let you know what develops."

Her voice was quiet. "Thank you. And be careful, won't you?"

I promised her I would. I looked in the mirror over the filing cabinet and decided there had been nothing personal in that remark. She was just a kind girl.

I phoned Rick Martin and asked him if Jackie had ever mentioned my suspect's name to him. Jackie hadn't, or Rick didn't remember it.

"Got something hot?" he asked me.

"Maybe. Have the Heffners bothered you lately?"

"Not lately. How about you?"

"Pug and I still have a title match coming up. But I guess it can wait. When is Jackie's funeral?"

"Friday. In Waukesha, Wisconsin. It's too much of a trip for me."

Or for any of her other new friends. I wrote up the rest of the day in my reports and went down to Cini's for some onion soup. And from there I went home and napped for an hour.

The house was older and smaller than those of his friends. It needed a coat of paint and the asphalt driveway was pitted and uneven. From the rear of the house he could see the finer homes of his wealthier friends and look down on the grave of Mrs. Quirk, and from that spot he could shoot the man he hated. The green Ford Club was parked in the driveway, so I could guess he was home.

He opened the door to my ring and studied me thoughtfully. "Is something wrong, Mr. Callahan?" The light from behind him seemed to halo his fine hair.

"I don't know," I said. "I'd like to talk to you."

"It's eight o'clock," he said. "I've a date at eight-thirty."

"With Deborah?"

His voice was quietly wary. "That's right. Is there any reason why I shouldn't have a date with Deborah Curtis?"

"I suppose not. You've loved her a long time, haven't you?"

He stared at me. "What do you mean? Why are you here?" His voice was firm, but I thought I could almost hear an edge of panic.

From the hall behind him an older voice said, "David, is something the matter?"

Keene called out, "There's nothing wrong, Father. I'm just talking to a—an acquaintance." He turned back to me. "Why are you here, Mr. Callahan?"

"To check a lie you told me. Do you want to sit in my car and talk? I don't want to disturb your father any more than I have to."

"This is ridiculous," he said evenly. "You're not a policeman, you know, Mr. Callahan."

"All right," I said, "I'll take it to the police then. They're better equipped for this sort of thing than I am, anyway."

I turned and started for my car.

He said, "All right. I can give you ten minutes. Is there a heater in your car?"

In the car, I turned on the heater blower and turned the interior lights on. I wanted to see his face.

He closed the door and asked, "Now, what was the lie I told you?"

"You told me you had never heard about Johnny and Miss Arness. But I learned that you were the one who squealed on them."

"That's not true," David Keene said hoarsely. "If Mr. Brockton told you that, he lied."

"Mr. Brockton wouldn't tell me," I said. "Miss Arness told me."

"Elin— Miss Arness? You talked to her?"

"For quite a while. She told me that you held her in very high esteem. She said it was uncomfortable to be revered as much as you revered her."

Keene said softly, "She was a saint to me. She introduced me to the most important thing in my life, good reading, good writing."

"And when she betrayed your idolatry you wanted to smear her, didn't you, and the boy who'd caused her fall?"

"No. El—Miss Arness is mistaken. She was never really mentally sound after what happened."

"That could be. And you? Were you? Is that when you started to hate Johnny Quirk, or was it before then?"

"I never hated him. I'll admit he didn't impress me much, but I never hated him."

"Yes, you did. And you knew he went to his mother's grave every Thursday evening. And you knew he was tied up with Jackie Held and Jackie was a friend of Rick Martin's. So you phoned Martin, pretending to be Johnny, and arranged the meeting for a place where you knew Johnny would be."

David Keene's voice was a whisper. "You're mad. Why would I do that?"

"Because you hated Johnny, and now you learned that Johnny and Deborah were finally going to get engaged. It had been on again, off again for years, but now it seemed definite. That would be the final straw, wouldn't it? You had put the note in Johnny's car as a red herring for the police and now you were finally going to eliminate him from your life."

Keene was breathing heavily.

I said quietly, "It would be an easy shot for the champion of the Beverly Rifle Club."

"You've nothing," Keene whispered. "Nothing, nothing, nothing. Talk, that's all you've got."

"Isn't that the story of it, David? This hate grew through the years, this hate for the arrogant athlete who was so much richer than you and so much more popular. This kid who'd despoiled your idol, this tomcat of a kid who was going to marry your girl . . ."

Some semblance of control in his voice now. "All right, I never liked John Quirk. Plenty at school didn't. Why don't you investigate them, go digging into their past and concoct another smear story?"

"Was Jackie trying to blackmail you?" I asked him. "Maybe Johnny told her you hated him. Johnny would have been sensitive to your feelings about him. He wasn't dumb. And maybe he told Jackie and she realized you were comparatively safe from the police unless someone pointed a finger at you. Where did you get the conine, David?''

"You may go now," he said quietly. "You've said your piece. You're not a policeman. Take your story to them, if you want to."

"All right. Do you sell used typewriters? I didn't notice when I visited your store."

"Good night, Mr. Callahan," he said. "I'm late now."

"Late for what? You intend to leave town, don't you? You want me to go, and you'll be a long way from here by the time I bring the police back, won't you?"

"Get them," he said. "Go and bring them. And prepare for a false arrest suit." He opened the door, and stepped out.

He was halfway to the house when the department car came up the drive.

Sergeant Gnup rubbed his eyes wearily and then reached one hand back to massage his neck. It was quiet and dim in the small room off the squad room. He said, "The boys will break him down. He's a stubborn kid. But we've got the print and it matches his."

"Not from Washington you didn't get it. Keene was never in the army."

"Who said we did get it from Washington? What point you trying to make, Callahan?"

"Only that without my pointing finger you wouldn't have had a suspect to match to the print. What brought you up the driveway at the opportune time, Sergeant?"

"Martin called and told us the name you'd asked him about. I guess Martin was afraid you could be bought."

"That's a nice thought."

"Typical from a Martin. What steered you onto the kid in the first place?"

"Because he pretended not to know something that *all* of Johnny's friends knew. I guess he was trying to steer me away from Miss Elinore Arness. Or else he had a psychic block about the whole horrible incident."

An officer came in, a man I didn't know. He told Gnup, "The kid had a rifle with a silencer. And there was an antique typewriter in that garage studio of his that looks like the one. Though I'm no expert.''

"Experts work the day shift," Gnup said. "We'll get one. Go in and relieve Jantzen for a while."

Gnup looked at me. "There are two reporters waiting in Remington's office. What do I tell them?''

I held his glance. "You can tell them that Private Investigator Brock Callahan of this town, working in close co-operation with Sergeant Gnup of the Beverly Hills Police Department, have solved the Quirk and Held killings.''

Gnup frowned. "Shouldn't that be 'has' instead of 'have'? How about opening with: 'Working in tandem'? I always liked that for an opening sentence.''

"All right," I said. "But be sure my name is spelled right.''

"All right, I'll tell them that." He rose and went out.

I went out to the hall and saw David Keene's father sitting on the chair near the doorway to the squad room. I avoided his eyes as I made my way to the wall phone.

Jan didn't sound sleepy. "Well, hello. I tried to phone you half an hour ago. No answer.''

"I've been working. Why did you phone?''

"To apologize. Moira Quirk came into the shop to explain. Wasn't that thoughtful of her? You told her about me, didn't you?''

"I drop your name a lot," I admitted. "What are you doing now?''

"Sitting here with six bottles of Einlicher in the refrigerator, waiting for a big, dumb guard to phone.''

"I'm on the way," I said. "I have a story to tell you.''

As I turned from the phone Gnup came over. "He's breaking down. Stay and hear it if you want.''

I shook my head. "I don't even want to read about it, Sergeant. Life's too short.''

"For some," he admitted. "Well, luck, Callahan.''

I went out into the cold night air and headed the flivver west, toward Beverly Glen. I hoped that damned Doberman wouldn't be out to welcome me.